W9-AAD-927

W9-BZP-138

To Hell
or the Pecos

Center Point
Large Print

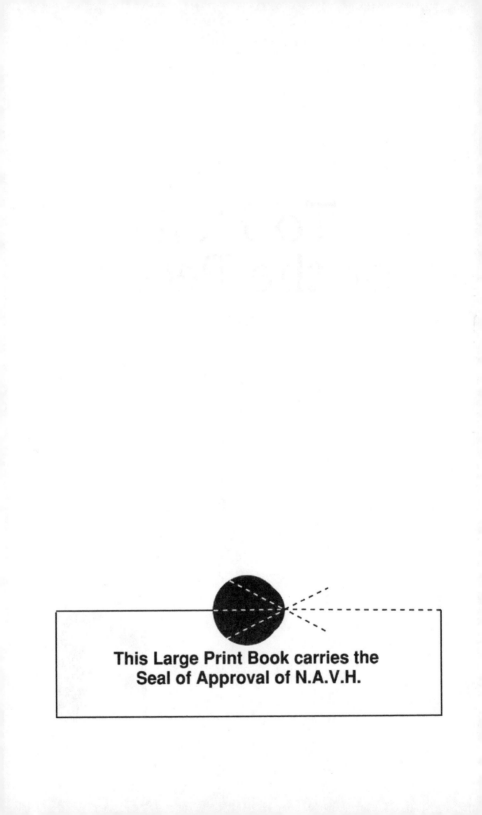

**This Large Print Book carries the
Seal of Approval of N.A.V.H.**

To Hell
or the Pecos

Patrick Dearen

CENTER POINT LARGE PRINT
THORNDIKE, MAINE

This Center Point Large Print edition
is published in the year 2014 by arrangement with
Texas Christian University Press.

The text of this Large Print edition is unabridged.
In other aspects, this book may vary
from the original edition.
Printed in the United States of America
on permanent paper.
Set in 16-point Times New Roman type.

ISBN: 978-1-62899-378-3

Library of Congress Cataloging-in-Publication Data

Dearen, Patrick.
To hell or the Pecos / Patrick Dearen. — Center Point Large Print
edition.
    pages ; cm
ISBN 978-1-62899-378-3 (library binding : alk. paper)
    1. Cowboys—Pecos River Valley (N.M. and Tex.)—Fiction.
    2. Cowboys—Texas, West—Fiction.
    3. Pecos River Valley (N.M. and Tex.)—Fiction.
    4. Texas, West—Fiction. 5. Large type books. I. Title.
PS3554.E1752T6 2014
813′.54—dc23
                                                        2014034525

To Elmer Kelton (1926-2009)

Nurtured by West Texas,
he wrote of its range and people
with insight and authenticity.

May his gentle ways
live as long as his books.

To Hell
or the Pecos

"When a bad man dies,
he goes either to hell or the Pecos."

—BUFFALO HUNTERS

ONE

Sarah!

How many times he had silently voiced her name. He had never spoken it aloud since that black hour, but how many, many times he had called it in his thoughts and dreams, through fitful nights and dawns such as this, breaking empty and alone and as gray as the ashes of his campfire.

Sitting cross-legged before the mesquite flames that lapped a smutty pot, he took the 1860 Colt Army revolver by the walnut stock and watched the smoke curl over the tarnished brass trigger guard and cylinder caked with rust. He ran his fingers down the eight-inch barrel, feeling the brief but distinct bulge, and re-lived the blood and foul gun smoke and ringing ears of that distant night when he had rammed in too great a charge in his haste to reload. In those desperate moments, he had never known for sure which round had ballooned that barrel, but now his mouth went dry and the .44 trembled in his hand at the idea that it had been the last shot—the round for which he had placed the muzzle gently beside her ear, deliberately slipped forefinger over trigger, thumbed back the hammer to an ominous click.

Tom Rowden swallowed hard, the years of regret,

and worse, exploding inside him like that final round must have done between those crumbling walls. Funny how his mind spared him those last few details—his finger squeezing the trigger, the hammer snapping forward against the percussion cap, the quick—and merciful, he had believed—end to it all. But the memory of her lifeless body was vivid enough, lowered into a shallow grave of alkali dust.

He lifted the .44 higher, its three and a half pounds strangely heavy before the glowing coals, and suspended it, a blur before his cheek. He curled his forefinger through the trigger guard and bent a sweaty thumb across the hammer. Closing his eyes, he could smell the axle grease sealing the cylinder chambers and feel the barrel nudge his hat.

Sarah.

He was always closer to her like this than any other way, the revolver a strange bond across time and distance. Yet, it was never close enough, not even when he slipped the muzzle under his hat brim, as he did now, and met the upright barrel with his hanging head.

Sarah, I'm sorry.

On that long-ago night, the barrel had grown too hot to touch, but in a few days the muzzle would be cool and tender against his temple, just as soon as he reached Horsehead Crossing and those blood-stained adobe walls where Sarah had waited for him all these twenty years.

And finally, he would have peace.

A horse nickered quietly from nearby, and Tom opened his eyes to 1886 again and glanced over his shoulder at his hobbled bay. The animal did its best to graze nubs of grass on the hard-packed ground before a line of yellowed pecans, stunted plums, and shriveled gooseberry vines crowding the Middle Concho River. Even after all these years, Tom remembered this flat as a favorite camping spot, in a good season. To the west, it was only a few miles to Centralia Draw, and from there, seventy-nine barren and waterless miles to Horsehead and the Pecos. But in this valley's narrows, the Middle Concho made an oxbow bend around a jutting bluff and caught Kiowa Creek flowing out of the north—two streams in a West Texas wilderness always thirsty.

Still, in this drouthy August—eleven months past the last rain, so he'd heard—Kiowa Creek had gone bone-dry, while fly-blown cattle carcasses bearing a 7L brand had turned the Middle Concho's muddy trickle into buffalo tea. Even over the clinging scent of wood smoke, the stench was almost unbearable.

It would have been a hell of a place to have asked Sarah to dip up drinking water.

Sarah.

He closed his eyes, searching for her again across the years, and finding her only when he dwelled on the touch of that upright barrel against his hanging head. He wondered if she would even know him today, or if the haunting remorse had aged him beyond recognition. If she were looking down on him from somewhere, down as far as hell, he knew what she would find under the stained brim of a gray-felt hat creased extra deep. Crow's-foot eyes. An unshaven, angular face burned dark by the sun and crusted with skin cancers. Deep scoring at the corners of a gray mustache. A lost man, looking every bit his sixty years, with a linsey-woolsey shirt buttoned to the top and duck pants stuffed inside high-top boots with mule-ear tugs at the sides.

And a gun hand unsteady, but not so unsteady that it would deny him his final moment at her wind-swept grave.

Buried in thought, Tom didn't know how long it was before a sudden commotion stirred him. But even as he opened weary eyes to the sunrise mesquites to find the vertical barrel of the .44 splitting three riders—two reining up ahead of an emerging chuck wagon and remuda, and the third to the side riding hard toward him through the rising dust—he was still in another time, another place. Sarah was there, her limp head bloodying the hollow of his neck. He should have ended it there. He should have slipped the muzzle up against his temple and ended it there, but a sudden voice was calling through the dawn. It was hallooing, asking if anyone was there, still alive, still—

"Name's Jess Graham, with the 7Ls."

Tom squinted at the sunrise bursting through the legs of a horse that stirred sand across-fire from him. Its rider was a silhouette through the gray smoke, but as the animal shifted, Tom found trail dust and tawny stubble in a lean, mid-twenties face stricken with the kind of paleness only the dead should have. And those blue-gray eyes—they almost seemed to look through him, burned by a vision of their own private hell.

A looking glass, thought Tom. *Me in a looking glass, every day of my life.*

"Mister," said the cowhand who called himself Jess, "you don't look so good."

Tom lowered the revolver. They'd told him that twenty years ago. Daylight had broken and those passing freighters had climbed over the adobe wall and told him that. He wondered if he would look any different those final few seconds, huddled one last time against those mud bricks with Sarah's memory and a cylinder rammed full.

Tom coughed; old alkali dust hung in his throat. "Never seen a man yet looked good in hell or a Big Dry," he rasped in a voice drained of caring.

He saw Jess take a deep breath, as if trying to steady himself, and nod to the revolver. "Man's got to be careful with one of those things." There was a long, awkward silence, and that peculiar anguish seemed to burn more intently in the cowhand's eyes. He laughed a little nervous laugh. "Guess you know that."

Tom searched for the worn holster, a black flap-top, beside the tin cup of Arbuckle's coffee and found it with the .44's muzzle. He looked up again and saw that Jess's eyes had followed the weapon, to fix now on the ash-powdered leather that hid it. Strange, how the cowhand continued pale, and how his rein hand trembled until he steadied it against the horn. Tom's own child—a son, maybe—would have been nearly as old now, but Sarah's hadn't been the only heartbeat he had stilled that black moment when he had last whispered her name.

"You comin' or goin'?" asked Jess. His voice seemed to quiver a little. He nodded back to the deeply scored ruts bearing east into the browning scrub mesquites. "Just pushed a bony herd downriver. Marked the whole forty-odd miles to San Angelo with dead 7L stuff. Headed back in this mornin'—the 7Ls is just three, four miles off-trail from here. You can fatten up plenty quick, if you're a mind, even practice tipping your hat. Seventeen and pretty."

Seventeen. That's how old Sarah had been when they had married, the two of them sitting in a buggy outside the preacher's house, nine childless years before they turned the bois d'arc wheels of their eight-oxen wagon into the ruts of a California-bound emigrant company at Texarkana.

Eighteen sixty-six, five years after ousted Yankee troops had turned the frontier over to the Comanches, and there they were, headed for a hostile wilderness, six wagons and seventeen people with little more than sunbonnets and hats to keep their scalps from dangling on some savage's trophy lance.

"Hell of a country for a woman," said Tom. He turned, remembering, and scanned the lacy-leafed mesquites and the point of the gray, rock-rimmed bluff signaling the way west.

"Hell of a country for anybody right now," offered Jess. "Didn't catch your name, mister."

"Answer to Tom."

"Surprised to run across somebody who's not countin' dead cows from between a horse's ears."

Tom tasted the stench and turned back. "Don't think that bunch was countin' many in the dark last night."

"Who's that?"

Tom turned a hand over in a half-shrug. "Midnight, little after. Some riders 'cross-river, talkin' Mex. Don't think they knowed anybody was around. Watered-up and crossed between here and the bluff. Sounded like they was headin' north, four or five horses."

"Up Kiowa?" asked Jess.

Tom tossed a mesquite twig into the fire. "Don't think they was well-intentioned. Talked about takin' some saddles, a quirt, off some ranch night before."

"You sure? You speak Mex?"

Still, Tom had no energy. "About enough to cuss, but I savvy a little."

Jess turned away with a wag of his head and looked back stern-faced. "Hell, we never have any trouble around here. Been six, seven years since even any Apaches, they tell me. Now, over on the Pecos, that's a damned bandits' hideout, I hear. But Mr. Buckalew—he's all stove-up—he and his daughter's by themselves at the 7Ls . . . right up Kiowa four miles."

Favoring one leg, Tom stood to stare in his eyes, then through the V formed by Jess upright at saddle horn and the long uplift of the horse's neck, he saw two roans approach, the nearer with a tight-lipped rider who picked at a flaring, alkali-dusted mustache. A couple of years Jess's senior and sitting taller in the saddle, he had a face oddly long and jut-jawed—almost horse-faced, thought Tom—with little pleasantry in the narrowed eyes or the veins that bulged at his flushed temples.

Grinding his crooked jaw, the quirt-lean cow-hand pulled rein, and Jess turned and quickly addressed him. "Sorrels, this man here says—"

"You spurred that horse over here like the heel flies was after you," interrupted the older hand, without even a glance at Tom. "Keep on sittin'

18

here gabbin' and that damned sun'll be high enough to give us sun stroke. I've seen it a-many a time."

Jess breathed sharply. "Don't get your tail over your back. This man here tells me some Mexes passed by headin' for the 7Ls in the night. Seemed to be up to no-good."

"Hell, just peons thinkin' they're cowhands. Down in the San Antone country they're thick as molasses." Then finally lifting his eyes to Tom, "Anyhow, I've got to disagree with you there, old fellow—you didn't see nothin', way that moon was all hid in dust last night."

The trailing rider, with a worn, leather vest and a flop-brimmed hat, pulled up alongside to tug at an earlobe and snicker. "Sorrels, if you was to stick your nose up under an ol' cow's tail where you couldn't see," he asked in an exaggerated drawl, "could you still smell somethin'?"

Sorrels turned, obviously agitated, and sneered at the freckled cowhand with bushy mutton-chops and scraggly red hair. Twenty-three or so, the latter sat grinning like a cowboy on his first visit to the kind of place no one ever spoke about in polite company.

"What the hell you smartin' off about?" Sorrels snapped. "I can whip a whole cow pen like you with one arm and guard the gate with the other."

The freckled cowhand only grinned more. "Just how big is that gate, anyhow?"

Tom knew this was no time for jawing, and he was damned glad when Jess spoke up.

"What Gabe's tellin' you, Sorrels, is there's more to knowin' than just seein'." He looked at Tom. "Heard five, six?"

"Not over."

"Yeah," spoke up Sorrels authoritatively, "the rhythm of ever' horse's gait is different enough where you can tell 'em apart sometimes. I 'member one time—"

"B-By gollies, Jess!" cried a kid-of-a-hand who held dusty horses beside the wagon white-loaded with bedrolls. He pointed excitedly to the north. "Hey, J-Jess! B-By gollies, you s-seen all that over th-there?"

Over the angular nose of Jess's chestnut horse, Tom looked through the upper fringe of wavy mesquites across-road and scanned a cedar-specked upland ending at sky and a smudge of gray. He cringed—for it stirred sudden nightmares of that attack at Horsehead, when he and Sarah had stumbled back over the bodies of women and children and fought their way to the adobe ruins of the stage stand. There, bleeding and helpless in the dying light with only a near-empty pocket flask of powder and a dwindling bullet bag, they had watched the Comanches throw the men up against the wheels of wagons out-of-range and lash them there. Then night had fallen, and the red devils had doused them with coal oil and set them—

"Looks like fire!" cried Jess.

"That's up Kiowa!" exclaimed Gabe. "What's left to burn in this boneyard?"

"Ain't prairie," said Sorrels.

"Looks like the 7Ls!" yelled Jess, whirling his horse. "Let's go!"

But Tom, the holstered .44 in hand, already was limping toward his own animal, his mind whirring with thoughts of two seventeen-year-old women and all the could-haves and would-haves of twenty years' past, had only somebody who cared come along just a little sooner.

TWO

Jess was troubled, damned troubled.

Up the side valley with its broken, gray hillsides, he rode hard, keeping to the trail that rimmed dead Kiowa except where its bank and brush line bent away from north. The unshod hoofs of his stocking-legged chestnut reached out again and again to catch bare ground or brittle clumps of grass and lift plumes of dust. This land was a burden for any grass-fed animal, but the burdens Jess carried inside were a hell of a lot worse.

Not for years had his father weighed so heavily on his shoulders, spurred by a stranger's grasp of a revolver. It had been a .44 cap-and-ball Colt the old man had held so close to that gray temple, just as Jess's crying father had done those seventeen years before when Jess had looked in through a crack in the shed wall. Jess had been only eight then, and maybe he couldn't have done anything to change things, considering the hell that had followed his father home from the war. Still, Jess had just stood and watched, and he would have to live with it for the rest of his life.

If he had just burst inside—hell, if he'd just said something, the way he had to the old man . . .

Jess had kept a lot of things bottled inside, all right, but even worse right now, he was damned spooked by what he might find up ahead. He had always liked old man Buckalew for his Christian ways, even though Jess had backslid a little since camp meetings as a kid in East Texas. But Buckalew wasn't the half of it—Jess was sweet on his daughter, Elizabeth Anne.

Like most cowboys, Jess generally longed to see new country after a season or two on a spread, but his feelings for Liz Anne, as her father called her, had kept him hanging on at the 7Ls ever since the rains had stopped nearly a year ago. For much of that time, she had been away at school, but now she was at the ranch house every day, although he seldom found a good enough excuse to drop by and conduct business with Buckalew. It was probably for the best, for all Jess seemed able to do around this only woman for forty miles was stammer like a damned fool.

But Jess figured he wasn't the only 7L cowboy smitten—he supposed it was the same with all the hands pushing hard up Kiowa with him. There was fun-loving Gabe, a few strides behind, often given to humor at inappropriate times but soberly polite around Liz Anne; young Dee back with the remuda, proudly apprentice-wrangling the horses while looking upon the older hands and Liz Anne with an impressionable sixteen-year-old's admiration; even scraggly Otie, probably cursing those chuck wagon mules with a buffalo skinner's vocabulary that never failed to melt into sweet innocence at her sight.

Sorrels, though, Jess wasn't so sure about, even as he kept pace a little behind Gabe. After all, he had even cussed an old bronc in Liz Anne's presence once and not apologized. Jess had let it pass that time, but he had always regretted not knocking his teeth in. Not only that, but Sorrels's lack of humility and common sense was down-right aggravating. Hell, a smart man knew better than to act the part of a know-it-all; the more a fellow knew about something, the better he ought to know just how much he had left to learn. For one thing, Sorrels hadn't caught on yet to the fact that the man running the wagon was Jess, even though Buckalew had made that clear.

Well before Jess reached the last shielding point

of rock, he struck the smoke that drifted down-valley. His eyes watered to the sting, but he could see the distant buzzards plainly enough, circling in the gray sky over a location that could only have been the 7L headquarters. There, just off Kiowa and under rim rock opening to a box canyon green with spring-fed live oaks, Buckalew had set up his first cow camp back in the '70s, so Jess had heard. For a year or two he had óverseen the operation from the settlement that became San Angelo, but as soon as he had built a modest box-and-strip house, a couple of sheds, and a mesquite-pole corral, he had brought his wife and young Liz Anne out to stay. But damn it, theirs had been the misfortune to get in the way of the last Apache raid ever in this country, and Buckalew and Liz Anne had been paying the price for it ever since.

In the last anxious moments of anticipating but not knowing, Jess pressed his horse a little faster through the fine ashes suspended in the air. They clung to his clothes like gray dust, the ominous pungency singeing his nostrils and sickening him like Otie's cook fire the time Gabe had slipped up in the dark and set it steaming with urine. That had been in prank, but there was nothing to grin about now.

Then Jess was in the last clearing and involuntarily reining up, stunned by a smutty rock chimney standing alone against rim rock, a chimney that rose up over a smoldering, charred mound whipped by the wind.

The 7L headquarters. The Buckalews' home. All that was left of a good family's dreams.

Like the chambers of a six-shooter discharging one after the other, details flashed rapid-fire. The currents lifted the ashes and swept them toward him, down the rock steps that dropped from nowhere, through the scorched limbs of a live oak, across a small yard landscaped with cacti, over a rock fence and on toward something black stirring at the base of the hitching post.

They were buzzards, perched on an angular form stretched out on dark-stained ground.

"Hyaah!" Jess spurred his horse and he was across the clearing, scattering the vultures into quick flight. The instant he was close enough to see for himself what he suspected—that the shadow tracks of their long, laboring wings retreated from the body of a man face-down and unmoving—he pulled rein again, suddenly scared as hell. He scouted left and right, looking for he-didn't-know-what. All he knew was that there was a dead man in front of him, and he was sitting there high in the saddle like a prairie dog out of its hole and every bit as vulnerable.

"He's dead, ain't he, he's dead." Gabe was beside him, as nervous as his skittish roan.

"They can pick us off like flies out here!" exclaimed Sorrels, reining up behind them.

Jess whirled again to either side. "Where? What do you see?"

"Maybe we oughta get out of here, Jess!" said Gabe.

Jess didn't need any more encouragement. He wheeled his horse and together the two spurred their animals away, turning Sorrels with them. Jess leaned forward to hug the chestnut, his cheek riding up and down with the foamy neck and his heart pounding like the drumming hoofs. Still, it was as if something awful was about to run him down, and he didn't hold the horse until he had managed a good hundred yards. Turning the chestnut, he tried to catch his breath in the stifling smoke as he looked between the two horses and riders pulling up behind him.

He saw the rock column again and the debris charred night-black, then the gray planks of the outhouse beyond, the mound and small cross under the rim rock. Off toward Kiowa, old wagon wheels and rusted irons leaned against the rough timbers that picketed the gable of a crude, A-frame shed. Against the live oak canyon stood the corral, its pole fence running snaggle-toothed into a tack house forming its west end. The sagging door screeched to and fro, the only movement anywhere except for the dust of their horses and the ashes on the wind.

Jess heard a commotion behind him, back toward the Concho, and he spun to see the billowing dust of the approaching remuda past the rock point. He turned again to the body in the sun, then caught Gabe's attention and nodded to the south.

"Why don't you go back and hold up those horses," he said in a shaken whisper. "No use that boy havin' to see all this."

"Mr. Buckalew won't be dishin' out powders today, will he, Jess."

"I don't know, Gabe."

But Jess did know, for on the crown of the dead man's head, he had seen a bald spot, just like the one Buckalew had always tried to hide under his hat.

Riding after the 7L hands, Tom passed the chuck wagon under a low bluff scorched with brown cedar and caught the remuda's dust, a hanging, powdery alkali that crawled down his throat. At his horse's breast, it fell like a fog over the nubs of grass tufts, and over gnarled deadfall and spider webs between the seared daggers of bear grass. To the side, it drifted over stubborn scrub-greenery—mesquite, catclaw, algerita—or over remnant foliage clinging shriveled to bony limbs. And all this under a sun beating down through a sky that looked as if it had never seen a cloud, especially west toward the Pecos.

The dead and the dying. Just like Sarah. Just like him.

He caught the remuda and its young wrangler just as the oncoming Gabe appeared out of the dust, his arm outstretched to the side as he pulled his horse out of its lope. Tom reined up, as did the jingler, to study Gabe's blanched face against the horses trotting on unchecked.

"Jess says stay put, Dee," Gabe said with a quake in his voice.

"M-My—"

Tom saw that the stuttering wrangler was only a kid, with a black-felt hat two sizes too big and a blue-silk neckerchief under a beardless chin caked with dust. Tom noted that the boy had a heady aroma—sweat, tobacco, manure—but then, he figured, so had he on all those drives up to Kansas in the '70s.

Dee pointed to the drifting remuda. "M-My horses," he finally managed. "M-Mister Buckalew won't be likin' me t-turnin' 'em l-loose that a-way."

Gabe looked down to find his hat band with his parted hand. "I don't think Mr. Buckalew's gonna be a-carin' no more, Dee," he said quietly.

Tom saw the boy's chin begin to quiver, then Gabe lifted his eyes and Tom found them and nodded up-canyon.

"What y'all puttin' your string on up there?" Tom asked.

"Nothin' we'll ever be sayin' 'fare ye well' to," said Gabe. It was a cowhand's adios to a lassoed steer that had broken free with a rope, or string, in drag.

Tom set his suddenly narrowed eyes up-canyon. "I guess I'll be seein'."

Not to be denied, he prodded his horse on past the cowhand blocking Dee's way.

He soon had the animal in a lope, on through the gray haze and around the point of rock to the clearing. Ahead, he saw the razed house and something under the hitching post, and the two hands studying the scene from afar. They turned in their saddles as he neared, and he found Jess ashen again.

"What about that girl?" Tom asked, pulling up alongside.

Jess's face showed helplessness. "I don't know. We're flat scared as hell, mister."

You don't know what in the hell scared is, thought Tom.

"There's a dead man up there," said Sorrels, nodding to the ruins.

Jess sucked in the stale air. "We didn't know who might still be up there ready to cause trouble. We didn't have anything to show we mean business."

Tom lifted the leather flap riding high at his left side. "I do."

Army-issue, the holster carried the 1860 Colt revolver butt-forward, and with a twisting motion of his right hand, he withdrew it and brought the muzzle across his torso and skyward.

29

"They'll pick us off like dogs out of their hole from that rim rock," warned Sorrels.

Tom set his eyes on the ruins. "Then maybe you better sweat this game from here—I'm findin' that girl."

Without any more hesitation, he urged his horse across the clearing.

With every falling hoof, Tom scanned the head-quarter grounds and rim rock with raised barrel, but all he could see were drifting ashes, ashes and the black of that long-ago night outside those adobe walls. They were out there, the devils. They were somewhere in the horseshoe bend's hard dark, just waiting for him to expend his powder. In a few seconds, or a minute or an hour, they'd come screaming in again and force him to fire his last two rounds. They'd do it, the red bastards, and Gabriel himself wouldn't be able to hold them off Sarah!

Two rounds.

One for himself, one for—

He found it suddenly just beyond his horse's breast, a body stretched face-down on the blood-soaked ground. It was a man, and the flies were blowing him where the vultures had shredded the back of his long johns.

Tom had seen death lots of times, from north-west Arkansas in the war, to the Pecos and hell in '66, to yet another lost year of utter hopelessness in the outlaw-horse country of South Texas. But he had never gotten used to it, never grown immune to the discoloration and the flies and the bloated stillness where there should have been life.

He looked over his surroundings one more time and dismounted in the smoke to stand with lowered revolver. He thought about Sarah, and about the man at his feet with a fine, gray ash settling across his shoulders like the shroud she never had. It was odd how the ants were drawn to the sticky ground, and how they massed at the man's neck.

He knelt and turned the corpse by the shoulder and saw why—his throat had been cut, and the dark-stained breast of his long johns and the thrashed ground all about told that his last moments had not been easy.

"Good God."

Tom looked around at the whispered oath and saw Jess shuddering astride the chestnut.

"Her father?" asked Tom.

Jess looked away with a nod.

Tom stood, shaking a little, the rage building inside him as it hadn't since he'd watched those red devils throw the men up against the wagon wheels. The sons of bitches had done this to a helpless old man—what would they have done to a girl?

"You think she's . . . Good Lord, you think . . . ?" Jess had turned back to motion to the smoldering debris.

Tom glanced back at Buckalew's body. "Not with him bein' out here."

Jess scanned the A-frame shed, the outhouse, the corral. "We've got to find her." Now there was as much anger as fear in his voice, and he set his eyes past Tom. "The corral, tack house. I'll be feelin' better if you go with me with that thing."

Gripping the .44 tighter, Tom mounted up and wheeled his horse with Jess's.

Jess found the pole corral empty and bloodless, but he was still plenty scared as he tied his horse to a raw timber and started after the stranger for the sagging tack house. He knew that Buckalew usually penned a pet horse or two when they came up to water at the spring every evening, but the gate behind him was swung wide, and Jess didn't know what it meant. Not only that, but he was in the open and could still feel something stalking him, and the slit of the door left ajar was dark as hell as it shrank and grew in the wind.

He didn't want to open it, didn't want to look inside. But there the old man was, with upraised revolver, leaning against the wall and swinging back the creaking door with a boot. Then Jess was at his shoulder, and together they edged around the jamb to smell old leather and stare at riding tack and the hands' nonessential belongings, stored here rather than in the wagon or line camps.

Again, bloodless. But there looked to be a roping saddle missing, and maybe a bridle.

Jess went in and came out unrolling a blanket holding a Colt Single Action Army revolver and a box of forty-one caliber cartridges. He'd had the 1873 model for years, long enough for the five-inch barrel to rust a little and the pearl grip to crack, but he had never worn it. When Sorrels had first signed on with the 7Ls, he had carried a Winchester under the stirrup, but only a damned fool like him would pack a firearm working cattle. Maybe in calving season when the loafer wolves got bad, there would be a reason, but the calf return was all but zero this year. Anyway, as Jess had told a disagreeing Sorrels, there was just too big a chance of his horse running into the brush and a limb catching it, not to mention the threat of a slack catch-rope or an angry steer's horn.

Jess stood in the glaring sunlight and loaded five rounds, leaving the firing pin resting on an empty chamber. He looked up to scan headquarters and again saw Buckalew's body, lying there in disrespect just as those SOBs had left it. Walking away in lock step with the stranger, he hung on to the blanket, and kept it as he mounted and turned his horse after the man's blue dun. But when the older rider continued on for the A-frame shed toward Kiowa, Jess veered for Buckalew's body and that awful, blood-caked throat spread wide under the uncaring sky.

He got off his horse and laid the blanket over him with a tenderness that didn't really matter anymore, and when he stood, he turned to the creak of a wagon and found Gabe, Sorrels, and Otie approaching. Waiting there, feeling so damned helpless, he looked over and watched the stranger dismount at the shed and check inside. With a knot in his throat, Jess studied him for a reaction that would verify the worst, but the old man was emotionless as he returned to his horse and mounted up. Jess breathed a little easier, but he didn't know what to make of the stranger's actions as he rode slowly away, for he leaned over the off-side of the saddle all the way to Kiowa.

Jess heard Otie's sudden oath at the blood-stained dirt, and he turned to see the chuck wagon pulling up, with Sorrels and Gabe ahead of the lead mules.

Jess chose to find Gabe's eyes alone. "They . . . They've killed her or took her off, one." He nodded to the tack house and corral. "Gate's open and there's a saddle missin'. What the hell are we goin' to do?"

"Yeah, they lit out soon's they killed old man Buckalew," said Sorrels, now suddenly as sure of that as he earlier had been unsure. "Probably find her layin' in the brush dead and her clothes tore off of her."

Jess turned to him, his face flushing hot. The arrogant so-and-so had a callous way of saying

34

it, especially with Liz Anne's father lying at his feet. He wanted to drag Sorrels off that horse and teach him some respect, but damn it, he was afraid he might be right this time.

Jess squeezed the grip of the .41 at his side. "Either way, we can't just stand here doin' nothin'." He nodded to the corral and tack house, "Liz Anne didn't ride off from here on her own—sidesaddle's still sittin' in there. I'm figurin' they throwed her up on a horse 'stride and she's still there."

Gabe had taken his horse to the body, to stare down and shake his head as his shadow played along the blanket. "Sorry we didn't come ridin' on in durin' the night, hollerin' like a bunch of yay-hoos on a drunk, Mr. Buckalew. I'm awful sorry we didn't." Then he lifted his gaze. "Sure hope you're right, Jess. Liz Anne—I . . . I can't stand thinkin' what they might've . . ."

Jess looked at him, sharing his fear, then caught peripheral movement and found the old man approaching with his horse in a lope, something small and white fluttering in his hand. Jess waited, wondering, then shuddered as the stranger reined up before him. *Good God,* he thought, searching those squinting eyes, *he's found her and her clothes, just like Sorrels said.*

Leaning over with a creak of leather, the old man handed it to Jess—a shred of cotton cloth, as might have come from a long-skirt chemise or other sleepwear such as he had seen in Miss Hattie's Parlor in San Angelo.

"Mesquite thorn caught it," said the stranger, with a nod toward Kiowa, "there where their trail climbs up out of the creek bed. They got her with 'em—didn't want her dead yet or they'd've done it here."

Jess whirled to Gabe. "Get back up there and help Dee bring those horses up—we got to rope out some fresh ones. Least, I do." He turned to Sorrels, and back again to Gabe. "Y'all's job with the 7Ls comes right up to here and stops. I'm not gonna be askin' anybody to go no further. I just know I got to, scared as I am."

The two men stared at him in silence for long seconds, then Gabe wheeled his horse but held it. "Hey, Jess," he said, looking around at him, "rope out ol' Clabberhead for me, will you?" Then he touched spurs to the gelding and was off.

Sorrels gained Jess's attention and nodded to the .41. "We go chasin' after 'em with no more'n that, we'll be layin' there dead as hell like old man Buckalew. I got a Meskin killer in there you'll be damned glad to see back under my stirrup."

He reined his horse for the tack house, but Jess hardly saw, for he was caught up in all he had to do. He faced the chuck wagon and Otie, who had sat cursing under his breath ever since he had seen the blood on the ground.

"Otie, I want you to turn that wagon around and

get started back to San Angelo, get the law involved in this."

"Can't ride no more, Jess, or I'd be a-goin' with you."

"I know. Otie, we're in a big hurry—do somethin' for me before you go." He nodded to the blanketed form behind him. "Give Mr. Buckalew a good buryin' over by his wife. He deserves it."

Otie glanced at the body and nodded. "I'll be makin' it damned deep, Jess," he said, urging the team on toward the chimney and the cross beyond. "Won't be no loafers diggin' him up."

Jess quickly mounted up and paused for a moment he couldn't afford, looking over his horse's ears toward Kiowa and the desert hidden behind the gray ridge under the sky. He couldn't get Liz Anne out of his mind. They had cut her father's throat and probably had done worse to her while he had bled to death in plain sight. They had thrown her up on a horse and headed her for Kiowa and that ridge hours ago, and God only knew what she was going through even as he sat here. Hell, he had to catch them—now!

"Started out like they's headed for the Pecos, the murderin' bastards," said the stranger, sharing his stare west.

Jess slung his head a little south of west. "Last waterin's the head of the Concho a few miles. If they take her on past there in this drouth . . . Good

God, I never had nerve enough to traipse off out there in a good year."

"You don't want to neither."

Jess turned and found the old man's eyes still fixed on the west horizon. "You been there, hadn't you. In this kind of a dry? What's off out there?"

"Hell," the stranger whispered hoarsely. Then he turned. "If you got a fresh horse, some airtights, I'd be obliged." He looked away again, lifting the barrel of the .44. "I'll kill the red sons a bitches."

Jess frowned and studied him, sitting there with raised revolver framed against the sky. "You said they was Mexes, not Indians."

The old man just tightened his grip on the .44 and kept up that cold, hard stare toward the Pecos, and still was staring when Jess reined his animal for the corral.

THREE

In a corner of roofless stone ruins as gray and empty as the breaking day, Liz Anne cowered by a mesquite shrub growing in the fallen rock and shivered despite the standing limestone's radiating heat.

Across the hours and miles, she could still see the blade of the bone-handled knife, dripping with her father's blood.

She denied. She grieved. She feared. But most of all, she grappled with a crippling sense of loss, mourning not only her father and her young womanhood, but all the innocence that the world had held for her just one short sunset ago.

All her life, she had known only good men. She hadn't known there was any other kind. Just men like Jess and the boys, who not only had looked up to her father, but who also had treated her with genuine respect simply because she was a girl becoming a woman. Just as important, she had felt worthy of that respect. But now, that was over, and she couldn't help feeling that she had done something wrong.

She could still smell his terrible odor all over her shredded chemise. She felt filthy. She wanted to die. She wished she had died, there next to her father in front of their burning house.

But God hadn't let her. While the unspeakable had been going on, she had reached for Him and found Him reaching for her, and He had spirited her away. It had been the only way she could have survived—by disassociating herself from her mortal shell and letting that part of her that gave her self-identity find safety in His care.

Now, if she could only forget. Forget the blood. The gurgling. The attack. The abduction. And all her dread of what might happen next.

She pressed her cheek against the unstable wall, wetting it with her tears, and glanced down along the quarry-marked rocks to the Mexican sitting back against the frame of a doorless opening. Ever since they had thrown her inside these grave-like walls far into the night, he had been there, grunting things that a good woman should never have to hear. He had grunted and snored and grunted some more, and all the while the muzzle of the rifle across his lap had pointed at her. In the dark, he had been just a squat, almost neckless shadow in a nightmare from which she had hoped to awaken, but now he was as real as the campfire smoke on past him, and the horses that stirred against the compound's outer stone wall, sixty or so feet away.

By day, she recognized the ruins by their size, twice her height where the rock hadn't fallen. She had been here once, or at least close enough for her father to point out the old stone breastwork, mortared with mud, and tell her he figured it for a stage stand in the Butterfield days. From the ridge to the east, it had looked more like a fort, the way its walls enclosed all but a large gateway just wide enough to admit a wagon and team. Crumbling and open to the sky, then as now, it rested on a slight elevation on the bank of the marshy North Prong—the Middle Concho "headwaters"—a few hundred yards from where the south-trending river bent sharply for the sunrise and San Angelo.

She looked again at the Mexican, dirty-haired and pig-faced, and found his bloodshot eyes fixed on her. She remembered him in the firelight of their torched home, standing and laughing while the skinny man with the shriveled arm had drawn the bone-handled knife across her father's throat. The squat Mexican had curled his deformed upper lip into a sneer and just laughed, and all the while, the blood had splattered his broad nose and fleshy jowls. The dried blood—her father's blood—was still caked on his face, and it made his stare so much more evil as he sat there, again grunting those awful things in broken English interspersed with Spanish.

Unfolding his short, thick legs, he slowly stood, keeping up the stare, and took a step toward her, then another. Liz Anne cringed, fearing but not knowing. *The boys will come,* she thought. *They'll not let this happen.*

He stayed framed in the open doorway as he took a third step, a fourth, his boots twisting into the loose rubble. Liz Anne came to her feet, already knowing there was no place to go even as she whirled around, a mesquite thorn catching her chemise. She turned again to the approaching Mexican and backed into the corner, feeling the rock bite her shoulders. *The boys won't let this happen to me!*

But it already had, in her father's very blood, warm and sticky beneath her at the 7Ls. And even if God should grant her escape now, what difference would it make? She would never be the

41

same. No husband would ever want her. She would never know a child's love. She would have only the memories, raging inside her every hour of every day, even if she somehow regained the will to go on.

She saw him come closer, and she closed her eyes against the uncaring dawn and prayed that he would kill her.

Stirring on the ground, his head in drunken repose on his outstretched arm, Lorenzo Perez awoke to find a tarantula crawling across his limp fingers. He had a foul taste in his mouth and a terrific headache, and he had neither the energy nor inclination to do more than watch the hairy, black legs work together to carry the spider over his thumb. They left oddly dainty trackways in the dust as they skirted the bottle before his face and mounted the cracked neck. Falling off the far side, the tarantula crawled away, but Perez's eyes stayed fixed on the almost-empty bottle, a glassy blur through his lingering drunkenness and the smoke that curled from nearby coals.

He had a foggy recollection of ruins and a compound and of falling here far into the night, and now a sudden whiff of the uncorked bottle reminded him that it was whiskey, taken from the house of the old man whose blood still stained his fingers. But strangely, in his half-stupor, it stirred memories of tequila, sloshing in a similar bottle for which a drunken, giggling woman was reaching.

She was a whore, but she was his mother, standing over him when he was six, her arm outstretched to the gray-haired man who held the bottle by the neck. She was reaching for it, there in that dark, smoke-filled dive in some forgotten adobe town as callous and colorless as the dawn now breaking, and the gruff-voiced *gringo* was holding it away from her. He was fending her off and nodding to Perez, nodding and bargaining. A boy, a bottle of tequila. A shrivel-armed child of *el Diablo* for a drink. Didn't she know that the whole village talked about him, this child born to the whore who had seen the six-striped lizard? Didn't she know it for the evil sign it was?

And then his mother was looking down and cuffing him on the head and pushing him into the old gringo's clutches. It was enough, she slurred, a fair trade to rid herself of this devil child who had brought her such trouble. Just give her the bottle!

What the tarantula could not do, the memories of seventeen years did. With a foul oath, Perez slapped the bottle away, slinging droplets of whiskey that pitted the dust all the way to the smoldering coals.

Groggily, he sat up and listened to the blowing and snorting of the others in drunken sleep—scar-faced Rodriguez beyond the coals, possessing a bandido's ambition and always begrudging Perez's authority in fuming silence; Rodriguez's one-eyed brother Ernesto, short in stature and temper, and even in siesta looking for trouble, there under the remuda lariat barring the gateway; Villa, given to thinking with his genitals instead of his head, in those crisscrossed bandoleers beside the stirring animals; and Luis, broad and swine-faced and not too smart, but smart enough to choose watch over the girl in a hidden room.

For eighteen months they had raided together, more out of convenience than loyalty. The others had allegiance to no one except their desires and Perez, who demanded it by the brunt of his personality and by firearm and knife. Subjected to every sexual whim of the old gringo for years, Perez himself loathed the concept of loyalty to others, especially those whose greed and lust he knew so well. Distrusting everyone and living in hatred of every viejo, old man, he sought only to dominate, just as the old gringo had dominated with horse whip and hand.

That is, until Perez had turned thirteen and opened the bastard's throat with a knife.

All across northern Coahuila, they had been satisfied with petty thievery and with drinking themselves silly in the arms of whores. But that had been before Perez had heard of a rich hacienda owner in Chihuahua who would pay mucho dinero for a young white wife. He didn't demand a virgin, but it wasn't a whore he wanted either. So Perez had decided to raid into Texas, where they had plundered here and there while looking for just the right señorita to bring the highest price. Then when he had least expected it, they had found the side-saddle in the tack house of the isolated ranch—reason enough to rouse the viejo and young woman in the night. Maybe she was more muscular than dainty, but at least she had a frontier femininity and an innocence about her.

That was, until Perez had let his desires get the best of him in front of the blazing house. Cabron! She had even been a virgin, evidently the old man's daughter, when he had thought her his wife. Already, Perez regretted lessening her value in the eyes of the hacienda owner, and all he could do now was make sure he wouldn't perceive her as worn merchandise. But keeping her untouched, when there were Rodriguez and Ernesto and the others—well, they had a long ride ahead, long enough for a lot to happen when there were five of them to split the money.

Any way Perez figured it, that was four ways too many. Maybe by the time they reached the Pecos and turned southwest for Chihuahua, he would find a way to whittle that number down a little.

Wiping his mouth where he had drooled in his

stupor, Perez turned quickly at a woman's sharp cry—a pitiful kind of cry that reminded him of a strung-up goat the moment a butcher drew a knife across its throat.

FOUR

Jogging along in the saddle, Jess moaned and readjusted the .41 hanging by its open loading gate in the waistband of his pants. Damn, it hurt, the way the trigger guard bumped his pelvic bone and the barrel probed his private parts every time the big bay reached out with a hoof. How was he ever going to carry the thing without tying it to the saddle, and what the hell good would it do there in a fix?

He felt the tug of scrub mesquite and catclaw against his leggings, which already were hot as the dickens even though the sun was barely two hours up. Wiping his streaming face into his shoulder, he fixed burning eyes on the spotted rump of the old man's lead appaloosa—Pretty Butt, they called it—and wondered if everybody else was as uncomfortable. The back of the stranger's shirt was dark with sweat, all right, but at least he wore his .44 in a flap holster, and Jess's quick glance back found the others almost as well-fixed.

There was Gabe on a brown-and-gray paint right

behind, with that Colt Hammer double-barreled shotgun—twelve gauge, he believed—hanging from the saddle horn by a thong loop. On a roan almost even with him was Sorrels, with the 1873 Winchester carbine, .44 caliber and twelve-shot, in a scabbard under the stirrup. But Jess was most struck by Dee's get-up, catching sunlight as he trailed on a leggy bay. It was a .45 Colt Peacemaker riding in a shoulder holster big enough to accommodate the seven and a half-inch barrel, an awfully big gun for a small kid-of-a-hand.

The Winchester and shotgun, Jess had known about, but Dee's revolver was a surprise. He guessed it was just as Buckalew had told him once: You wouldn't think a soul in camp had a weapon, but let trouble start and every mother's son would come up with one.

Jess's biggest surprise, though, was at himself, for letting Dee talk him into coming along. After all, he was just a boy, and a backward one at that. But he fairly worshipped the ground Liz Anne walked on, and that's why Jess couldn't see making him stay put. Anyway, it damned sure didn't hurt matters that he packed that extra Colt. He just hoped that if he ever had to get at it in a hurry, it wouldn't bind in the pouch or get caught up in his armpit. Jess had heard that shoulder holsters were bad for that sort of thing.

But, damn it, he would have given a month's pay to have had one just like it right then.

They all had firearms, all right, but Jess couldn't help worrying that maybe they were getting in over their heads. After all, they were chasing the kind of men who would stop at nothing, who had done the unthinkable already and wouldn't hesitate to again. And Jess, like most cowhands, minded his own business and never went looking for trouble. Hell, he'd never even been in a fistfight, and he'd been cowboying since he was fourteen.

Gabe, meanwhile, was, well, Gabe. A good-natured old boy. Aggravating at times, with all those jokes and pranks, but damned sure no killer. And what the hell good would Dee do, even if he could yank out that .45? He was goosey and unsure of himself even with the remuda, and he sure didn't have any business being here.

Then there was Sorrels. A big talker, for sure, and contrary and even downright mean. "Boys," Buckalew had warned, "these horses belong to me from the girt forward and they're yours from the girt back." They had all understood—lay off the club and don't spur in the shoulders. But Sorrels still openly worked the iron-loaded butt of his quirt between the ears of an unruly horse, and those crisscross scars on his roan's shoulders sure hadn't come from mesquites.

But those were horses, for God's sake, not men ready to slit his throat.

The stranger alone seemed to have the gumption

it took. But he was just an old man, with a bum leg and a mind that seemed to be somewhere else half the time. Not only that, but Jess strangely kept seeing him beside his father across a campfire, their heads hanging against gun barrels, and he didn't know if it was backbone the stranger had or something far more cowardly.

One thing was sure, though. He knew how to track, and when he pulled rein and held up a hand as they neared the rim rock at the divide's west edge, Jess knew to stop his bay dead in its tracks.

The old man was staring, and Jess took the chance to scout things for himself. He saw the nearly mile-wide valley in shades of gray, darker along the brushy L-track of the bending Concho, lighter along the gently sloping folds of the two hundred-foot ridge across. Away to the southwest, the tableland gave way to an intersecting valley almost as wide: Centralia Draw, the west-bearing old road a linear blight of alkali in its brush-darkened floor. But what struck Jess most was the crumbling rock fort, shining in the sunlight before the stream course and teardrop marsh overgrown with yellowed reeds.

Jess looked at the stranger and saw only that same unwavering stare. Bringing the bay up astride of the appaloosa, he found the old man shivering, the squinted eyes clouded by he-wished-the-hell-he-knew-what, especially with Sorrels grumbling about him under his breath.

Jess nodded to the Concho brush line halfway across the valley.

"Last waterin'," he told the stranger. "A bunch headed this way would be gettin' pretty dry by now. Up in the night like it was, I'm figurin' they was lookin' to hole up, get their horses' bellies full. I'm figurin' they liked the looks of those old walls."

Only now did the stranger turn those crow-track eyes to the crumbling ruins. But still he did nothing but stare, even more intently if that were possible.

"I'm figurin'," repeated Jess when he got no response, "we oughta be damned careful checkin' that fort out."

Only now did the old man seem aware, though his gaze stayed fixed on the valley.

"You'd be figurin' right," he rasped, and pulling his .44, he took his horse on down through a gravelly chute in the rim rock.

Finding his own revolver, Jess urged his bay after the old man's appaloosa, and from behind, he heard hands fumble with rifle and shotgun and six-shooter as three sets of hoofs slid down the same talus.

At the valley floor the rubble gave way to a dusty flat thinly scattered with mesquites no taller than a calf. On through prickly pear and tasajillo,

Jess kept his bay in a walk, a stride behind the puffs of alkali rising at the appaloosa's hoofs. At the mounds of a corral-bare prairie dog town, Jess looked down and read for himself the tracks of the night before. Lifting his eyes, he found the limestone ruin prominent through the scrub brush ahead, and as every pace took him closer, his pulse quickened.

Good God. There might be flesh and blood men in there, men he'd either have to kill or let send him to his own shallow grave. And anyway, how the hell were they supposed to go about this? Just go riding in like damned fools and wait for a rifle to pop over that wall?

Maybe Jess didn't have the smarts, but he reckoned the old man did, for just before they got within rifle range, the appaloosa veered left from the on-threading trail.

Jess turned with him, staying at Pretty Butt's hindquarters through brittle grass nubs as the old man bent slowly around toward the Concho's sparse brush line, never closing inside of four hundred yards of the ruins the whole half-mile to the first pool.

Pulling rein, Jess found the Concho headwaters more marsh than river or spring, its broad, dirty shallows afloat with green lily pads. He looked upstream, finding more lilies and marsh, and studied the breastwork away to the northeast. The compound's south-facing gate was open, but even with the changing angles incurred by their half-moon ride around it, he had seen no movement, no horses, no men—but that didn't mean there weren't any.

Plagued by self-doubt, Jess was still trying to figure out how to get inside without catching a bullet when he heard the stranger splashing his mount across the marsh.

"Where the hell's he goin'?" snapped Sorrels, who had pulled up alongside to pick at his flaring mustache. He slung his hand to the northeast. "That trail was headin' straight as hell for them walls. That old man must be blind as a bat."

Or cagey as a coyote, thought Jess, watching the appaloosa gain the far bank and turn upstream, still maintaining that four hundred-yard buffer against rifle fire from the breastwork.

"Give him a chance," said Jess.

Still, Sorrels grumbled.

Gabe, holding his horse at the salt grass on the bank, found Sorrels's eye. "Maybe it's like you havin' your nose under that ol' cow's tail—he can still smell plenty."

"J-J-Jess," spoke up Dee, preempting a spirited exchange between Sorrels and Gabe, "y-y-you think Liz Anne's in there? We-We goin' after her, ain't we, J-J-Jess?"

"We're goin', Dee, but sometimes it pays to find out all you can about an ol' bronc before you climb on him."

But as he took his horse into the marsh's lily pads and splashed on across, he wondered if he was heeding his own advice when it came to the rider in the lead.

Letting the appaloosa pick its way upstream along the brushless bank, Tom stared again and remembered.

Away to his left, between gray ridges, the valley of Centralia Draw yawned wide, its scrub brush signaling the way to the far-off Pecos just as it had twenty years ago. Up the draw, he could still see in his mind their wagons curving around the jutting point two miles away, starting their slow, labored climb up yet another drainage trending from the west. He could see the water barrels sloshing full, but not full enough, and see the cattle, their bellies bloated with water, moving along almost contentedly, never knowing that only the strongest would drink again, endless hours of day-and-night hell away.

He could still hear the teamsters shout Gee! and Haw! and could catch the pop of their rawhide whips as they walked alongside the ox teams. He could distinguish the creak and groan of the trailing wagons, and could hear the kettles and pots rattle to the jolting road, while trudging women and children filled the possum-bellies under the wagon beds with mesquite-root firewood for next camp at the fuel-less Pecos.

He could still see it all: the herders and teamsters and women and children, walking the last, lonely miles to their graves.

He could still see Sarah.

Then he turned and looked across the stream with its yellow reeds and thin brush line at the walls of native rock, bone-white in the sunlight. It was funny how it seemed only a year or two since he had been here, how, even now, that breast-work still stood like a marker to hell.

Within a revolver shot of it they had made camp, and for two days they had burned wood from its fallen roof and let their animals water and graze and water some more. They had rested and waited, men and animals delaying the inevitable, then on the third afternoon the oxen had pulled at their yokes and the wagons had lurched forward, leaving those mortared rocks to watch the final passing of all those good people.

Now Tom was back, twenty years later, alone even if others rode with him. And that same breastwork, just as uncaring, was watching his own final walk down that dark, lonely trail from which nobody ever returned.

Veering off the stream course, Tom continued a slow bend around that fortified station, always just out of rifle range across the river. Three hundred yards toward a bulging point in the west ridge, the gray-nubbed grasses gave way to old wagon ruts, left and right. Dismounting and holding to the reins, he knelt and traced a finger over horse tracks between the scoring.

"Headed west. And fresh."

He looked up at Jess's voice and found that the cowhand had pulled rein next to the appaloosa. West, all right, thought Tom, turning again to the trail. And plenty fresh. That much anyone could tell.

But Tom could tell more. He could read just how long it had been since those horses had passed. If the tracks had been made in the night, they would have been filled with tiny insect trailings—and they weren't. Scanning the ground, he found where a hoof had cut the blade of a horse nettle, and judging by how little it had dried, he knew that it had happened no more than ninety minutes ago. By the depth of the tracks, he could count not only the horses, but the riders, and there was something damned disturbing in what he saw.

He stood, staring back over the appaloosa's nose at the rock ruins in the sun, but now he saw only far-off walls of adobe, standing as the only marker for another woman's grave.

"You know somethin', don't you," said Jess with a quiver in his voice.

Tom winced while keeping up that fierce stare toward the walls. "Six people rode in to there—and only five of 'em rode out."

He turned to Jess and saw him go pale again as

the cowhand wheeled his horse for the ruins, taking the trailing riders with him. Tom, delayed by mounting up, was the last to turn his horse back up the road for the ford and that damned tomb-of-a-fort one hundred fifty yards beyond. He had just urged his horse into a lope when it suddenly hit him—a quick, crippling sensation in the chest, as if he had been roped from behind. It was like a band around him, as broad as his hand and squeezing like hell.

He slumped over the saddle horn, knowing he had to get off and lie down but realizing he wasn't able. It was the third spell he'd had in the ten days since he had told the boss of that South Texas cattle outfit to figure up his time, and he didn't know how many more he had suffered in those last few weeks of trying to make a hand in a job where a man was old at thirty-five.

Usually, the incapacitating constriction at his chest would ease after three or four minutes and leave him none the worse for wear. He hoped to hell this one wouldn't be any different—he didn't think a man could stand it if it lasted any longer. If he could just count off the seconds—sixty, a hundred, two hundred—it would be over, and maybe he could get that much closer to Horsehead Crossing before the next one caught him.

After all, it had been these very spells that had finally made him realize that if he was ever going to make peace with himself—even the kind to be found at the muzzle of a .44—he had better do it damned quick.

Tom's horse fell off the pace, and then stopped altogether where the wagon ruts dropped off into the marsh. The tightness in his chest lingered, but he managed to lift his head up along his animal's neck and see the receding 7L riders framed against the skull-white walls, and he dreaded like hell what they would find in there.

FIVE

Jess had not felt this way since he had stood at the shed door with the gunshot ringing in his ears and watched his mother burst inside crying his father's name.

He knew the vision of hell waiting past those walls.

He was through the gate and into the empty compound, tasting the smoldering campfire and the horse manure and swinging off the bay even as he pulled rein. The dust rose up to choke him like his sudden emotions, and it hung in the air against left-side ruins broken three times by onetime doorways. He scanned them left and right and quickly back again, something white and fluttering catching his eye through the middle entrance.

Good God.

He whirled around, a creeping fear again coming at him from all sides. Gabe and Sorrels were at his flank, reining up, and outside the gate was a troubled Dee who had pulled rein to sit white-faced and winded by nerves on a horse just as skittish.

Jess, too, seemed to have a hard time getting a breath as he tied his reins to a quarried slab at his feet, and when he straightened quickly, everything went black. He shook it off and turned again to the inner ruins, his temples pounding. From his perspective, the doorway was just a jagged slit—*like hell opening up,* he thought—but across the ruins he could still see the low-lying garment, waving in the wind like a white flag in surrender to what-had-to-be.

Lifting his .41 to the sky and slipping a quaking thumb over the hammer, he went closer, suddenly unaware of anything but that garment and the anger rising in him. It was a blind rage that he had never felt before, fueled by deep-rooted hatred—for himself for his inaction at that shed, for his father for denying them a life together, but mostly for those sons of bitches who had killed Buckalew and dragged Liz Anne off in here.

They'd killed her, the bastards! They'd killed her, and damn them to hell, what could he ever do about it?

He reached the crumbling doorway, and he saw the chemise clinging to a mesquite shrub near the back corner and had to steady himself with a hand to the rock jamb. With each whipping gust, the garment revealed, then hid, bare skin in the background rubble, under whitewashed walls stained dark with blood.

Good God, he couldn't go any closer. He hung his head and lowered his .41 and just couldn't go any closer. He had watched his father squeeze that trigger and had seen Buckalew stretched facedown in a sticky pool, and now to find a girl who had deserved such respect—who'd had his respect, and so much more—lying there violated and dead in all her innocence was more than he could take.

A shaken Gabe suddenly was at his shoulder. "What's in there, Jess?"

Jess looked up and just shook his head.

Sorrels was there too, gripping that Winchester, peering inside at the garment and body and bloody walls.

"Just what I figured," he commented, brushing past to crunch rubble. "Let's get this over with. No use them flies blowin' her any more than they got to."

Jess hung his head again and stared blankly. What if they had rounded up those cattle one day sooner or pushed them a little harder to San Angelo? What if they had gigged their horses a little deeper on the way back? What if they had ridden in last night instead of holing up on the Concho?

They could have done it. Any of it. All of it. And it was all his doing, all his fault, because he was wagon boss and he alone had made every damned one of those decisions.

And Liz Anne was dead because of it.

"What . . ." His reluctant voice was broken. "What do we do now, Gabe? What the hell do we do now?"

"I suppose we give her as good a buryin' as we do the loafer wolves a supper—soon as we catch up to 'em."

"Hey," called Sorrels from across the ruins. "Looks to me like them loafers can start with breakfast right here."

Jess flushed hot and found Sorrels stooping over just past the chemise. He wanted to shoot the SOB. He was standing there gawking at Liz Anne's body naked and violated, and hell, Jess just couldn't believe that even Sorrels had the disrespect to make that kind of remark.

Gabe must have read Jess's face, for he quickly found his shoulder with a hand. "Don't get worked up over him, Jess. You know how Sorrels is sometimes. You could rake hell with a fine-toothed comb and never find a sorrier man."

But Jess's rage mounted as Sorrels continued to study the body from up-close. "Get your damned hands off of her, Sorrels! If you're not takin' part in the buryin', just get your damned hands off of her!"

Sorrels looked back over his shoulder. "I ain't diggin' a hole for this greaser, I'll tell you that. If you want to, have at it."

Jess exchanged glances with Gabe. What the hell—

Jess bolted across the rubble to look past the chemise and Sorrel's hip at the all-but-naked body in the sun. God Almighty, it was a *man's* body, squat and almost neckless, lying there in the blood-splattered rocks with a hole the size of a silver dollar where his thick, oily hair massed in back of his head. Turning, he found Gabe alongside, every bit as stunned. Then the two ran back into the compound, spooking the horses and setting Dee to stuttering a quick question he just couldn't manage.

Jess looked down the inner wall to the ruins nearest the gate, then gestured to the farthest.

"That other room, Gabe—I got this one!"

Jess ran for the first breach, spurred by a single thought: *Six people had ridden in here, and five had ridden out.* He reached the opening and burst wide-eyed around the jamb, hoping like hell the stranger had counted right. He brought the barrel of his .41 swinging down across sun-drenched walls, leveled it on mesquites and jumbled slabs, checked left and right to find only fallen rock in the near corners.

Six people had ridden in—

"Gabe!"

"Nothin' here, Jess!"

Liz Anne and four others had ridden out.

The pain in Tom's chest was gone, but he had a hell of a lot of worries still on his mind as he pulled his horse out of its lope where the 7L riders gathered outside the gate.

"The girl?" he asked immediately, searching for, and finding, Jess's eyes through the rising dust.

For once, there was color in the younger man's face. "She's not there. Thank God, she's not there."

"Not—?" Tom quickly looked at the ruins. "You didn't see, couldn't've missed—"

Sorrels chuckled. "Well, there's a Meskin dead as hell we had a hard time missin'. Naked with the back of his head blowed off."

"But the girl—you didn't see no sign of the girl."

Jess nodded to the walls. "Her sleepwear's there. I figure she's in a dead man's clothes, but . . . *good God, she rode out of here.*"

Tom closed his eyes against the sunlit breastwork and measured his relief against his festering hatred. They didn't kill her. They didn't because they weren't through with her. They'd do to her what those savages would've done to Sarah!

Jess turned his horse west toward the crossing. "We've got to ride hard. We've got to catch up with them before they—"

"You can't charge hell with a water bucket," said Tom, and his calm, authoritative tone caused Jess to hold the big bay. Tom looked squint-eyed toward the far ridge and the canyon that opened in the southwest. "You gotta be ready for it. I'm tellin' you, it's a helluva country out there, a helluva place to be afoot. I expect we better rest these horses a little, make sure they're watered up. Once a man crosses that creek, it's a Big Dry clean to the Pecos."

"L-L-Liz Anne," spoke up Dee. "Th-They ain't a-hurtin' her, are they, J-Jess? Th-They ain't a-hurtin' her right now, are th-they?"

"Been just a hour or two since they rode out," Tom went on. "They rested them horses half the night and they got a extra one now, case somebody's gives out. Right now, from them tracks, they ain't much ridin' like the heel flies is on the chase. I don't think they's figurin' on anybody comin' after 'em.

"We rest these horses just a hour, give 'em a good waterin', we'll still be ridin' drag, but we can be close enough to sling a cat-gut on 'em 'fore you know it." He turned to Jess. "We stay smart about this, we can get that girl back. We end up afoot with give-out horses, that poor girl's good as . . ."

Jess hung his head. "We've got to go now," he argued, barely above a whisper, "keep those SOBs from . . ." A long sigh passed his lips, and he nodded to the crossing. "We'll rest 'em over there, drink our fill."

"You won't hear me makin' a kick about it, way this sun's beatin' down," said Gabe.

Sorrels snorted and urged his horse for the crossing. "Just what I was figurin' on doin' all along."

Tom saw the frustration and anxiousness in Jess's face as the young man turned to the waiting desert. "In just a little bit, son," he told him, sharing his stare toward the Pecos. "Just a little bit and we'll bust her in spite of hell."

And I'll be with you, Sarah. I'll be with you!

SIX

Ever since sunup, they had been following a trail of dead men.

It was late morning, and the sky burned with a quiet fury that could make more men dead damned quick. Over his shoulder, Jess measured the sun's fiery swell through the rising dust, then he turned again to his bay's nodding head and the rutted road ahead. The horse tracks were still there, leading them on into a country about as inviting as hell, just as the old man had said.

It was an all but gray hell, from the caked alkali that powdered with every falling hoof, to the stunted and almost bare mesquites, catclaw, and algerita in the rocky drainage flanking their course. Only here and there were traces of color: the cactus hues of spiny tasajillo, bear grass daggers, and shriveled prickly pear; the orange or green tint of an occasional rock painted with lichen; the brown of scorched cedars dotting the slopes. Even the sky was gray, dusted with that same alkali that crawled down Jess's collar.

It was a high sky too, thought Jess, one that seemed to start low on all sides and climb a hell of a long way up, swallowing him as it went. It gave him a sense of smallness, and even though he wasn't alone, he suddenly felt a lost, lonely figure riding in a sea that just went on and on with nothing else in it.

The stranger was right. It was sure no place to go wandering off into with just a wish and a hope.

What Jess hoped right then was that he and the others had what it took, that their horses had what it took in this wilderness where a man was no better than his mount. For thirty minutes now, they had kept them in a jog-trot, that steady gait that could eat up a good seven miles an hour. But that was when there was water and forage and rest waiting—and there was damned little of that where they were headed.

As for themselves, Jess knew they had awfully little in the way of supplies. He longed most for a canteen, but a cowhand who worked with the wagon didn't know what one was, and only a tenderfoot ever complained about a dry throat out of sight of the chuck wagon barrel. Right then, though, with the sun wrenching the sweat from him with his every bounce in the saddle, Jess wouldn't have hoorawed even the greenest-broke hand for making a kick about being thirsty.

At least they had a few airtights along, mostly tomatoes canned in water. Already, he wished for a swallow, but with that horizon waiting up ahead cloudless and sun-broiled, he knew he had to go sparing on his liquids. Even the muslin sack of tobacco in his shirt pocket had shrunk a little, but in the pouch on the side of his saddle, he packed a reserve of tobacco, stuffed in his canvas war bag along with .41 cartridges, a spare shirt, socks, and a change of underwear.

The saddle pouch also held his leather poke and last month's pay, but the more he thought about Buckalew's bloody throat and Liz Anne's shredded chemise, the more he wished he could trade it all for just a few more cartridges.

"Say, Jess."

Jess turned to the horse trotting at the hind-quarter of his bay and saw Gabe pat the paint on the neck.

"If ol' Clabberhead keeps a-hoofin' it like this all mornin'," said Gabe, "I'll be like ol' Bill Murphy they sing about. You know, 'Ol' Bill Murphy was a good ol' boss, but he went to see the girls on a sway-backed hoss.' "

The stranger suddenly was bringing his appaloosa up on the outside of the paint, and as soon as the old man lifted squinting eyes to Jess, Jess knew to wait and listen.

"Son, I expect he's right about easin' up a little. Get more out of these animals if we change our gait ever' so often."

"What I been tryin' to tell you," spoke up Sorrels from the roan behind Gabe. "A hand ain't much to brag about if he don't know his horses. I 'member one time I—"

Ignoring Sorrels, Jess looked back at his own animal and the lather white and foamy on its neck, and he knew that the stranger was right, no matter how badly he wanted to push hard after those murdering dogs. He eased the bay into a walk, slowing the other riders by his action as the dust came sweeping up from behind.

They went on at that gait for a minute or so, and as the dust cleared a little, Jess looked back for Dee. He had fallen thirty or forty yards off the pace and was riding along, tilting his too-large hat first one way and then another as he studied his shadow over the off-side of his leggy bay.

"Look at King Solomon back there, Jess," said a grinning Gabe with a nod back. "Reckon we oughta road-brand him 'fore we lose him?"

Sorrels breathed sharply. "I don't know what in

the hell you let that kid come along for anyhow. If he ain't slowin' us down, he'll be gettin' in our way."

Gabe looked at Sorrels. "You're so surly this mornin', if you was an ol' bronc, we'd have to tie your hind foot up to get on you."

"Still say he ain't got no business out here," Sorrels continued. "Oughta be back on the farm drivin' turkeys."

Jess remembered Gabe's advice back at the ruins; with all the things going on, Sorrels wasn't worth getting worked up over.

"Dee's all right," Jess said. "Just got some growin' up to do, same as some men."

"Yeah, well," said Sorrels, too busy berating to realize the insult, "I've seen a-many a kid roll that bedroll up and go home to mama."

"Dee don't have a mama," reminded Jess. "Father neither. Never knowed him to speak of any family at all."

"I'm tellin' you," pressed Sorrels, "them Meskins will cut him up for calf fries, mama or no mama. If it'd been me, I'd've figured up the kid's time a long time ago."

Jess flushed hot. "I'm tired of hearin' it, Sorrels."

From the appaloosa surging past, taking lead, the stranger cleared his throat, drawing the three men's attention. "Where I come from," the old man offered, keeping his eyes fixed ahead, "if a man comes across an unbranded yearlin' not

68

followin' a cow, he takes him home and looks after him."

Then the stranger pushed his horse ahead a half-dozen lengths before again easing it into a walk.

"Helluva place he's got smartin' off," grumbled Sorrels. "We'll be havin' to nurse-maid him same as we will that boy."

"I wouldn't go bettin' my wages on that," said Jess. "Appears to me, he's holdin' his own pretty good."

"Yeah, well, so's ever' steer in the herd till the drive gets goin'."

Out of the corner of his eye, Jess saw Gabe look back at Sorrels with an exaggerated turn in the saddle.

"Tell me if I done got mixed up on my directions or somethin', Sorrels," said Gabe with a snicker, "but 'twixt you and him, ain't you the one playin' drag to his lead steer?"

A few minutes down-trail, the stranger pulled rein ahead of the 7L riders. Sorrels grumbled under his breath as he halted alongside Jess and watched Tom rub his bad leg.

"Old man's done give out like I knowed he would," Sorrels said indiscreetly, drawing a glance from Jess.

But now Tom was pointing toward the folds of the small hills ahead, bringing Jess to study the distance. The old man must have had eyes like an eagle, to see the wisp of dust low in the sky, while

Sorrels had all the savvy of a bull around a herd of cows in heat.

"Kind of dust you'd expect of a bunch of horses," Jess pondered.

Only now did Sorrels evidently spy the faraway puff of haze. "Got mustangs in these parts. One time I throwed my loop on one and damned near—"

"I'd say forty, forty-five minutes ahead—and right down the road," interrupted Tom. "They's in the right place at the right time to be those SOBs, all right."

"We-We gonna ca-ca-catch 'em?" pressed Dee. "We-We g-gonna ca-ca—"

"We's sure enough on their coattails, Dee," said Gabe. "Sway-backed horses and all."

Jess had heard enough talk as he fixed all senses on the distance. "Let's get 'em—let's get 'em *quick*."

Only the stranger's outstretched arm kept Jess from gigging his horse.

"They's bad *hombres*, son, plenty bad," said Tom. "We don't need to go buryin' any more good men today than we already done."

This time, Jess was determined to follow his instincts. "We gotta go—don't you understand? They've got her. They've got her and we gotta ride 'em down."

"We are, son. But we wear these horses out tryin' to close on 'em, won't have nothin' left by the time we can get 'em in our sights. Like as not, they ain't seen us yet. We keep these ponies in a fast walk and hold our dust down, got a decent chance to be in shootin' range 'fore they ever look back. These parts, fresher horses mean ever'thing."

No, thought Jess. *Liz Anne means ever'thing.*

But he was glad one of them could look at things without emotion crippling his judgment.

As they rode into midday and on into afternoon, gaining little by little on that wisp of dust, Jess didn't like what he found in himself.

He was afraid they might never catch those riders, and just as afraid that they would.

In Jess's eyes, the worst a man could be was a coward. What difference did it make if he could tussle with an ornery steer or run his horse all-out in a black-as-pitch stampede? What about facing a man down, muzzle to muzzle? How the hell had his father ever done it in the war?

But maybe that was part of what had driven his dad inside that shed so many lonely years ago.

Jess checked his fellow riders, wondering if they were any less scared. As the miles had tolled by, Sorrels had said plenty about his prowess with a carbine, but the tic of his cheek and his shifting eyes betrayed his bluster. Gabe's jaw was no less hard-set, about as far from a grin as Jess had ever seen it. Dee, still bringing up drag, repeatedly glanced back, as if worried that an unseen

71

menace was about to snatch him from the saddle.

Damn it, thought Jess, fear itself would kill them all if they let it. It would rattle their nerves and steal their breath and send their shots wide. Tom alone seemed to ride with self-control, but maybe this stranger who had seemed to seek solace at the barrel of a .44 back at that campfire faced a greater demon than any of them.

In Jess's search for courage, two words, then four more, ran roughshod through his mind.

Liz Anne.

My life, for hers.

Still, a part of him wanted to do nothing but wheel his horse and spur it as far from that swelling puff of dust as possible.

He needed desperately to focus on something other than his self-doubt, and when Sorrels checked the magazine of his Winchester, Jess found it. Sorrels alone carried a rifle, giving him a decided advantage in range over Gabe's shotgun and the revolvers of everyone else. With a glory seeker like Sorrels—the kind who would shoot first and consider the consequences later—the dangers to Liz Anne were grave.

"You ain't to go shootin' that thing till we're on 'em!" Jess shouted. "You hear me, Sorrels? You ain't to go shootin' till we know which one's Liz Anne!"

Sorrels pulled rein as his neck went crimson. "What the hell you hollerin' about?"

Jess maintained his bay's pace. "Liz Anne! She's in a man's clothes. Don't you forget it!"

"Expect he's right," spoke up Tom, his voice calm and assuring. "Anyhow, best thing might be to take their horses out from under 'em. A helluva bigger target, and settin' 'em afoot out here's same as killin' those red savages."

Jess exchanged glances with Gabe, and even with Sorrels, before looking back at Tom. The old man suddenly seemed even older, the way he squinted those crow's-foot eyes at the horizon, and all of Jess's doubts magnified like that branding-iron of a sun in the sky.

Despite the ever-present glare, a gloom settled over Jess as they pushed on up a nearly mile-wide drainage in the shadow of two-hundred-foot bluffs. As if the situation wasn't ominous enough, bands of whitewashed rim rock hung over him like scythes, while the road ahead was gray and lifeless and marked by bones with drawn and decaying skin clinging in tatters. Jess had seen enough buzzard pickings the last several months to become callous to the sight of dead livestock, but the smaller, half-buried bones they sometimes passed raised the hair on his neck. If he had any doubts as to their nature, the makeshift wooden crosses told him all he wanted to know.

If ever there was a valley where death was more than a shadow, this was it.

The drainage squirmed as it carried them

through a virtual hell, and in mid-afternoon the road veered toward right-side rim rock and stayed, subjecting the riders to radiating heat as they hugged the looming bluff. They bent with the folds of the ridge in a miles-long arc, and all the while the cacti-studded slope concealed the way ahead. For an hour or more, the column of haze down the road remained as hidden as the north sky, then Jess burst around a point a little behind Tom and abreast of Sorrels to face a greater test than he could have ever imagined.

Not a hundred fifty yards past the nose of Tom's appaloosa were five figures, trudging on foot and leading their horses away through skeleton valley.

"There!"

"By gollies!"

"Son of a—!"

"L-L-L-L-"

Gabe and Sorrels joined Jess in barely contained cries, but Dee still was stuttering when Tom yanked his 1860 Army Colt out of its holster with a cross-body sweep. Even as he brought the eight-inch barrel skyward, he spun to Jess with words ready on his lips.

They never came, for sunlight flashed in Jess's eye and he found Sorrels shouldering his Winchester.

"No!"

Lunging, Jess clipped the rifle barrel as it boomed. The discharge boogered Jess's animal, and he was still half out of the saddle as the shying bronc downed its head. Falling forward along the horse's neck, he somehow weathered a couple of jumps as images flashed like light through a spinning revolver cylinder.

Five whirling figures. Tom's appaloosa. A bordering ridge that was there one moment and gone the next, vanishing in a furious sandstorm that had burst over its summit.

The five figures down-road disappeared too, and from out of the sudden dusk at Jess's shoulder, Tom's appaloosa reared and leaped into a gallop.

Digging spurs into the bay's hide, Jess managed to pull its head up and draw his .41. Racing the animal through a pile-driving wind, he could taste the grit between his teeth and feel the sting of his violently flapping shirt. Then a howling darkness fell and the sand filled his eyes, smothered his nostrils, choked his throat. He couldn't breathe or cry out or find escape, and panic seized him. All he knew to do was protect his face with his gun arm and keep his terrified horse on as straight a course as possible for where those figures had vanished.

Barreling through a purgatory that seemed to have no end, he couldn't even guess where Tom and the 7L boys were, and after the longest minute of his life he realized that he should have already overtaken the figures in the road. Maybe the Mexicans had taken to the saddle and fled, or maybe he had ridden just a little wide and over-shot those murdering devils. Either way, he was now so disoriented that all he could do was press on with a backslider's prayer for a seventeen-year-old girl, and a second one for himself.

Push! he cried silently. *All the way to the end, for Liz Anne!*

Then the darkness broke a little and he lowered his shielding arm to face a pair of looming, brute-black shapes dead ahead. At the last instant, his squealing horse planted its forefeet, but still a half-ton of man and animal plowed broadside into a moving form.

The jarring impact dropped the bay to its knees and drove Jess across the saddle horn. As he winced to its bite in his kidney, he felt the drag of a rope along his neck. Parallel to the ground, it stretched from one brute form to another, and through the swirling dust he made out a lead horse and then a second animal, trailing at rope's length. As the latter figure swiftly brushed past with its rider, Jess thought for a split second that he could see a face as stunned and terrified as it was girlish. Then the dream-like images were gone, lost in a storm as seething as the one inside Jess.

"Liz Anne!"

Jess's cry died in the dust that hung in his throat. He somehow stayed in the saddle, but even as his bay regained its feet, he searched for another glimpse that just wasn't there.

Wheezing and wiping his eyes, he turned the bay in blind pursuit and found himself riding into the very teeth of the shrieking storm. The fury was more than man or horse could take, and when the bay cold-jawed and reared, Jess knew he had no choice. Reining his mount away from the wind, he gave the animal its head and buried his face in its neck.

Battered and rocked by an unstoppable force, he clung there frantic and helpless, wondering if he could endure one more second of this—and wondering even more what the consequences would be if he couldn't.

SEVEN

Tom had never seen such a storm.

He had ridden in stampedes in which the roar of hoofs had exploded from billowing dust that had devoured entire cattle herds. He had faced lightning and pummeling hail and torrents of rain that had spawned flash floods on the open plains. He had even survived a Kansas cyclone, a dancing, black rope that had fallen from the sky to kill a fellow drover and a hundred steers. But never had Tom experienced the kind of unadulterated anger that now gripped skeleton valley.

He huddled on the ground under his horse's breast, his hand firm on bridle and reins as the frightened animal tried to jerk free. It was a sorry excuse for a windbreak, but it was the only one he could find in this end-of-time judgment. In his other hand, he still gripped his .44, but he couldn't help wondering if he would last long enough to put it to use at those blood-stained adobe walls on the Pecos.

The wind screamed like a panther, and screamed some more, but still a man's muffled cry pierced the tenuous veil at Tom's shoulder. He turned, catching the hint of a horse-sized shadow surging by, at its base a dark, bouncing wisp in violent chase. Tom's appaloosa dodged, almost ripping the bridle from his grasp. At the same instant, the wisp grazed Tom's boot, then rolled and tumbled onward until it seemed to stop mere yards away, even as that greater shadow vanished in the devil winds.

Tom had seen only glimpses, but he was cowboy enough to piece it all together. A bronc gone wild had thrown its rider, and a stirrup or lariat had seized the victim's foot to drag him alongside the pounding hoofs. Now the boot had worked free, and lying out there bruised or broken or dead was either friend or fiend. No matter which, Tom's response had to be the same, even under these worst of conditions.

Cocking his revolver, he tugged at his horse and

urged it about, then bore straight into the blasting sand in search.

The appaloosa slung its head in fierce opposition, adding to Tom's exhaustion as he fought his way forward like a drunk weaving through a Kansas cow town. He would gain a step only to lose two, but finally he inched his way to within a couple of feet of a shrouded figure sprawled facedown with an arm extended. Here at ground level the dust raged even more, if possible, the drift building against the body's windward side. Such details Tom could make out, but he couldn't even hazard a guess as to the person's identity until he reached down with his gun hand and found crisscrossed bandoleers on the chest—and by then it was too late.

Like the strike of a rattler, a hand darted out and clasped Tom's leg, felling him like a fore-footed colt.

He lost the bridle as he slammed hard into the ground, but a cowhand's instinct led him to keep a death grip on the reins. It may have been all that saved him, for as a body hard with muscle fell upon him, the appaloosa wheeled from the storm and dragged Tom free.

Faced with a hopeless dilemma—hold fast to the reins and maybe catch a hoof in the skull, or let go and allow the superior strength of youth to finish what it had started—Tom chose to hold fast. He plowed through the dust for several yards before the cow pony stopped, but now an even graver threat gripped him.

In his chest came that quick tightening, the cinch-like constriction crippling enough to drop an ox. It heightened by the second, choking his very will, even as he saw the Mexican butcher descending on him again in search of reins and horse and the life that would go with it.

Sarah! Tom cried silently. *They's on us, Sarah!*

He was back at those mud walls at Horsehead Crossing, a savage face suddenly in his own as he caught a flying body. The force was punishing, driving Tom backward and crushing him against earth. But even as he grappled with that demon, fighting over battle axe and revolver and Sarah, Tom counted. He had fired one shot, a second, a third. But what about a fourth, or even a fifth? He, they could only carve up and mutilate and burn alive, but Sarah . . .

Sarah! Had he already spent all but the round he must save for her? Or could he afford to try to work that muzzle in close and—

His .44 roared at point-blank range, now as it had then, and the Mexican fell away, relieving Tom of the burden upon his chest but doing nothing to ease the greater one inside. The appaloosa shied and dragged him by the reins another several feet, then mercifully halted to leave him doubled up in the wind and sand. As a gloom more dreadful than ever descended over skeleton valley, Tom clutched at that agonizing cinch across his breast, but mere fingers were futile against something they couldn't even touch.

The way that inner strap seemed intent on squeezing the very life out of him, Tom didn't need a sawbones to tell him that this spell was the worst he had faced. He knew he couldn't stand much more, but he had no choice but to keep his grip on those reins and tough it out.

Either that, or die.

Right now, the latter would have seemed a blessing had he not already set a date at Horsehead Crossing with the ballooned barrel of an 1860 Army Colt.

Liz Anne longed for death, and wondered if she already had found it.

The witching dark, the wraith-like wails, the tomb of suspended dust through which she whirled in such torment—was this not hell? But what of the saddle beneath her, the stirrups around her feet? The dead had no need for a mount, yet she peered over the shadowy ears of a horse, while just ahead loomed the hazy hindquarters of a lead animal.

There was even more to ponder. Through her nightmare world had just floated a strange image of her father's foreman and most trusted hand, another reason to question this as a place of punishment. If ever there was a good man, one who had shown her father such loyalty and herself such respect—and more—it was Jess.

Even if she no longer deserved it, because of—

With a choking gasp, she sank to the crushing memory of a filthy man's face in hers outside her burning home, and she knew that death's precious escape was still all too far away.

But might she now have reason for hope? Maybe Jess and the boys really were here to take her out of this horrible hour. But how could they when, with what she carried inside, her life from this point forward could only be a living hell?

She could never face Jess again, never face herself after what that devil's spawn on the lead animal had done to her. It didn't matter that his bullet had stopped a second violation of her womanhood back at that stone breastwork; one right could never erase the unthinkable evil he had already perpetrated against her and her father.

There was only one thing left to do. She slid from the horse with a prayer that Providence would see fit to take her from this awful world.

She didn't know what to expect when she hit the ground, but it was something other than the piercing pain that met her hip, ribs, arm. She cried out involuntarily, recognizing the spiny thorns of prickly pear and tasajillo even as she cowered in quivering fear that the shrivel-armed man on horseback had heard.

Through an onslaught of wind and grit, she

thought she saw the ghost horses halt, then she turned and scrambled to her feet. She fled the storm and fell clawing at the ground. She staggered and stumbled onward only to drop again, a mere toy in the merciless blast. This time, she kept low to the ground, crawling over rocks and cacti that gnawed at her out of the dark. She managed to clamber to all fours before another brutal gust rolled her, and now as she struggled back to hands and knees, it was only to plummet forward.

Had there been sky it would have spun as she tumbled down what her senses told her was a sharply cut wash. Her fall couldn't have lasted more than a few seconds, but the blackness made it a terrible plunge that seemed to go on and on before she found herself hugging a steep bank that protected her from the storm.

Abruptly night gave way to ghastly twilight and she looked up past a ledge to find the sun blood red—moments before something at bank's crest blotted it out. Even before she recognized the silhouette of a horse's nose, she was digging nails into dirt in a desperate climb toward a rock shelter up under the ledge. A horizontal keyhole, it was tantalizingly close, but so too must have been that shrivel-armed rider who would deny her death.

Kicking and praying, she gained the dark recess and squirmed inside. It was shallow, just large enough to accommodate her slender frame, and it reeked of a sickening, almost metallic odor that singed her nostrils. There was an odd familiarity about that smell, and it filled her with dread at a time when she thought herself incapable of feeling anything anymore.

She caught quick movement outside and abruptly discerned the forelegs of a horse drop from the overhead ledge and plant themselves in the unstable slope at her face. She recoiled as the hoofs slid downward, and just as the girded underbelly of the gelding came into view, maracas vibrated wildly at her elbow and something slithered across her thigh.

Snake den!

Liz Anne may have consciously longed to die, but the instinct for self-preservation still controlled her reactions. With a cry, she dived into the open, shedding rattlers that somehow missed.

But now she was under the hoofs of not just one horse, but a second, each of them shrinking from the staccato of rattles. Hoofs pounded the turf about her head, midriff, knees, but succeeded only in grazing the hollow between her neck and shoulder. Within moments, the lead animal broke into frenzied pitching that forced its rider to give up the tow rope of the trailing pony. She glimpsed the shrivel-armed man pulling leather as his mount carried him on a frantic ride down-slope, but she was more interested in the dragging reins that now danced in her face.

Lunging, she seized them and held on long

enough to gain her feet and clutch the cheek of the bridle. She had learned to ride before she could walk, her father had said, and her time away at school had done nothing to diminish her abilities. Maybe she would have been more comfortable with a sidesaddle, as all proper ladies were expected to utilize, but she had enough experience on deep-seated roping saddles to feel confident as she found horn and stirrup and swung up astride.

She brought the bay under control, and horse and rider angled down to the wash's rocky bed. The shrivel-armed man had his hands full with a bronc determined to dislodge him, and as his terrified animal bolted left, Liz Anne reined her mount in the opposite direction. Visibility was still poor and the arroyo was rife with pitfalls, but she never hesitated as she kicked the gelding into a hell-bent run.

The hoofs drummed in concert with the wind's mournful cry, and although the dust whorls were blinding and the footing loose enough to cause her horse to stumble, she kept the animal in devil-may-care flight. For a moment she felt hope, but it was hope built on the knowledge that the bay's next step might land her in her father's faraway new home.

They raced on and on into an ever-shifting curtain of sand, the horse repeatedly breaking stride but somehow negotiating the abrupt bends. She could feel the hammer of its heart through her legs, and she admired the way the animal gave its all for her, just as her father had done in the flickering light of their burning house.

All of a sudden her senses whispered of new danger, and she spun in the saddle to find the shrivel-armed rider at the limits of visibility only a few yards back and gaining fast. No! Oh, Papa, no!

Whirling again to the ominous unknown ahead, she leaned forward and patted the bay's neck, begging the animal for speed it just didn't have. Within a few strides more, the pursuing horse came abreast and an arm lunged for her reins. She slapped it away and gigged the bay harder, succeeding in gaining half a length only to lose it just as quickly.

For a full minute the two horses ran almost side-by-side, faltering and surging as their riders continued their desperate joust. Again and again the shrivel-armed man reached for reins or bridle, only to grasp empty air as Liz Anne veered the animal sharply away. Once, he managed to seize her arm, but she sank quick teeth in his wrist and he released his hold with an oath. Lust or greed worthy of Satan's brood may have guided his ways, but Liz Anne fought with the passion of a girl who wanted only the right to die.

Suddenly an eroded butte rose up dead ahead and split the two of them, funneling Liz Anne's horse up a fork on the right. The arroyo quickly narrowed and began to steepen, but at least for a moment she had left her pursuer behind. There was a lot of slippage and the bay was weary, but she could still feel the animal's power as it bore her up through a V and out of the drainage.

The instant Liz Anne topped out to face the furious wind, three pivoting horses exploded out of the storm directly in her path. With a squeal the bay reared, so unexpectedly that it yanked the saddle out from under her. As she tumbled backward, powerless to do anything but let the inevitable happen, she glimpsed the cruel faces of a pair of demon-seed riders who would deny her merciful death just as surely as would their shrivel-armed capitan.

EIGHT

Nightfall cast a foreboding stillness over skeleton valley, but enough dust hung in the air for the rising full moon to burn scarlet behind Jess.

He rode slowly after his shadow, never catching it, as he searched the muted desert for more than his eyes could see. A scrub mesquite here and an angular tasajillo there, a bear grass stalk on his left and a prickly pear stand to his right—these he could discern, but the desert gloom failed to yield its greater secrets.

His emotions surged like that awful storm through skeleton valley. He fumed about Sorrels's premature shot that had given the Mexicans warning. He cursed the luck that had darkened the land at just the right time to provide cover for their getaway. But most of all he raged against those butchering whoresons who had carved up Buckalew and still rode free with Liz Anne.

The sons of hell! He'd ride them down if it took until his dying day!

An orange glow still lingered in the western sky as he rode upon Tom. At the hoofs of his appaloosa, the old man sat with his head hanging against the barrel of his revolver, the same pose with which he had met Jess through the smoke of his campfire that morning. Whether suicidal or pensive, Tom's demeanor raised the same pangs of regret inside Jess as before, the same haunting guilt for having held his silence at that long-ago shed.

"You all right?" Jess asked. "Tom, you all right?"

Just as the old cowhand began lifting his eyes, Jess saw a crumpled figure a few feet beyond in the moonlight. Startled, Jess pulled his .41 out of his waistband as his heart began to race. But Tom seemed unconcerned; after a glance in Jess's direction, he again found apparent comfort in the touch of that revolver barrel against his forehead.

Jess took his horse closer to the crumpled form and stepped off. The bandoleers shining in the moonlight told him plenty, and the sticky mass that clung to his boot as he nudged the rib cage told him everything else he needed to know.

Stunned, Jess turned to the old man and found his pose unchanged.

"Lord, Tom, you killed him. He done bled out and died right here."

"They's more," Tom rasped without looking up. "They's comin' again and these walls can't stop 'em."

Jess stared at him. The stranger was losing it. Here they were, facing the worst kind of trouble on all fronts with Liz Anne's life on the line, and he was flat losing it.

But hadn't Tom succeeded where Jess had failed? What had Jess accomplished during that storm, except cling to his horse and wait? In the meantime, this bum-legged cowhand had faced off against one of those Mexican butchers and left him in a bloody pool.

Jess went to the stranger's side and laid a concerned and admiring hand on his shoulder. The old man was about the age his father would have been now, had Jess only spoken up all those years ago.

"He hurt you any, Tom?"

In answer, Tom began to rise with a deep breath and a hand across his chest.

"Somethin' wrong?" pressed Jess. "You breathin' all right?"

As the old man gained his feet, he took his appaloosa by the bridle and scanned the moonlit desert to the west with a squint as pronounced as if it had been broad daylight. When he didn't answer, Jess spoke again.

"I saw her, up close. Just for a second, but I know I saw her."

Now Tom turned, but he didn't respond until he once more faced the darkening horizon. From the distance, a wolf had begun to howl.

"They's down to three. Three of 'em that's bad as they come."

"We gotta go after 'em," said Jess, joining his stare. "They still got her, she's still alive, and we gotta go after 'em."

"Can't pick up a trail till daybreak," the old man offered. "Seen our bunch?"

Jess hadn't, not since he had spurred his horse into a gallop just as that storm had struck. "Figure they hunkered down somewhere, same as me."

"We've got to have them guns of theirs." Tom nodded to the western gloom. "Come daylight, we're puttin' spurs to these ponies and not stoppin' till we get them wolves fed."

Tom's grit and resolve continued to surprise Jess. This wasn't some 7L hand smitten by a young woman's charms; he was a total stranger seemingly without a horse in this race. Jess knew it wasn't a drifter's way to volunteer more than his name, if that much, and in his duties as wagon boss all Jess ever expected of even a new 7L hand was honesty and a hard day's work. But this aging man came across so mysterious, maybe even haunted, that Jess couldn't help wondering about him.

One thing was sure—Tom's gumption and drive to rescue Liz Anne rallied Jess's spirits just as they had begun to ebb.

Tom began to ungirt his saddle. "Better let these horses rest much as we can."

"Tom, why you doin' this?" asked Jess.

The old man looked around, his face quizzical in the moonlight. "Gonna need 'em bad, farther we go."

"I don't mean the horses." Jess set about unbuckling his own saddle cinch. "How come you helpin' us this way?"

Tom seemed to start, as though struck by a picture he wanted to forget. Reeling a little, he clutched his horse's mane and shook his head, as though trying to clear his senses.

"A man can't undo what's already done. Got tomorrow, that's all."

Jess had more to ask, a lot more, but now he held his tongue. Whatever troubled Tom, it must have been powerful, and sometimes the things a man kept hidden inside could drive him a lot farther than anything he might share.

Within spitting distance of the Mexican's body, Jess slept the first shift, his head resting against his saddle and his horse secured to the horn. The first inkling he had that trouble was afoot came when the animal jerked the stake rope so strongly that Jess's head bounced off the ground.

He sat up startled, his thumb on the hammer of his six-shooter. Both horses were going crazy, doing their best to bolt, and as Jess located Tom's upright silhouette and saw him pointing, he understood why.

Just a few yards away in the moonlight, the wolves were feeding on the corpse.

Jess jumped to his feet and seized the stake rope. "Good gosh, Tom, they're right on top of us!"

His sudden outburst startled the wolves, driving them back into the shadows, but Jess wasn't finished. "Let's back these horses out of here!"

He didn't wait for the old man's thoughts on the matter. He took up his saddle and led the frightened bay back toward the moon that still blazed a pale red. Buckalew, the most educated person Jess had ever known, had once told him that wolves would never attack a man, but Jess wondered if the wolves had ever been told. Anyway, who was to say to what lengths starvation might drive a predator in a Big Dry like this? And what about hydrophobia, which always seemed to rage in a drouth?

A full hundred yards away, Jess set his saddle down and re-staked his horse. A little shaken, for more reasons than he could count, he wanted to roll a smoke, but he knew that a burning ember on even a moonlight night was an invitation for a bullet.

Before long, Tom joined him and the two of them sat on their saddles and watched the dark figures return to the Mexican's remains. Jess's stomach began to churn, the way it had when he had looked down at Buckalew, and he turned away.

"We should've buried him, Tom."

Out of the corner of his eye, Jess saw the old man flinch. "Tied 'em to the wagon wheels, burned them poor men alive," Tom whispered. "Wasn't nobody showed them any mercy."

Perplexed, Jess studied him in the muted light. "Who, Tom? Who was it set somebody afire?"

Tom turned to him with those characteristically narrowed eyes and only now seemed to realize that he had spoken aloud. "Better get some sleep, son. I'll be wakin' you 'fore long."

Jess realized he was right, but even as he stretched out and closed his eyes, all he could see was a pack of snarling wolves waiting patiently as flames engulfed a screaming man lashed to a wagon wheel.

The next thing Jess knew, something was nudging his shoulder and he was looking straight up at an overhead moon.

"Get your gun—somebody's comin'," whispered Tom.

Jess groped for the weapon and panicked when he couldn't find it. He had fallen asleep with the revolver across his chest, but now it eluded his frantic sweep. Even as his fingers finally closed on the grip, his pulse continued to surge.

He came to a knee and pivoted. Tom had stepped behind the appaloosa, using the animal as a shield as he scanned the night back toward the east. Jess, in an exposed position, dived over his saddle and flattened himself. Lifting his .41 up along the pommel, he looked down the barrel at the outline of a single rider approaching.

"J-J-Jess? Th-That you, J-Jess?"

The pleading voice out of the midnight held plenty of fear.

Jess relaxed his gun hand. "Over here, Dee," he called, as quietly as possible.

Rising, Jess stepped forward with Tom and waited while the youth brought his roan into camp.

"You by yourself?" Jess asked as Dee pulled rein.

"It-It was plum' aw-awful, J-Jess," the rider half-sobbed. "I-I couldn't see n-nothin'."

"Bad on ever'body," said Tom, securing the pony by the bridle.

"You gotta watch who you go ridin' up on out here," warned Jess.

He wanted to chastise him more, knowing that the boy could have been killed, but he held his tongue when he saw Dee's distraught face as he swung down. His cheeks glistened in the moonlight, and it was clear from his quaking jaw that he was fighting to keep his emotions in check. A little uncomfortably, Jess placed a reassuring hand on his arm.

"Let it go, young fellow," said Tom. "Sometimes it's better to go ahead and just bawl it out."

Jess's caring touch and Tom's words of experience were enough for the young cowhand to release all of his pent-up emotion. He hung his head and broke into sobs that racked his slender frame.

Jess had no siblings, but he opened his arms like an older brother and Dee readily fell into his embrace. Jess had been so wrapped up in the horrors of the day and in what Liz Anne might be facing that he hadn't stopped to consider what all of this might be doing to a mere boy like Dee. For the first time, he questioned whether Sorrels had been right about leaving the teenager behind.

When the sobs stopped, Dee slipped out of Jess's awkward hug and lifted his head. "S-Sorrels t-told me one time a hand sh-shouldn't oughta b-be a-cryin'."

Jess flushed hot, remembering Sorrels's tooquick shot. "That so-and-so don't know ever'thing. You seen him or Gabe since that storm hit?"

"Th-They was there one m-minute and g-g-gone

the next. I-I just been wanderin' and afraid I-I'd never find n-nobody again."

"That's what you been doin' since you was ten years old, ain't it, Dee," Jess said compassionately. "Just bouncin' from pillar to post ever' since your ma died."

The moment Jess said it, he was sorry, for the boy lowered his gaze and seemed ready to tear up again.

"Appears to me he done found a home in the saddle," spoke up Tom. "You been doin' some mighty fine ridin', young fellow. Bet you're a-makin' a pretty good hand already."

Jess appreciated Tom's attempt to bolster Dee's spirits. "You bet he is," he agreed. "He's on his way to bein' a top hand one of these days."

The truth was, Dee was a backward kid who was more hindrance than help on the range, but Jess knew him to be a hard worker who always tried his best—something Jess couldn't say about Sorrels. What Dee needed most was a shot of confidence, and the way he lifted his head and beamed at their words, Jess figured Tom's comments had accomplished more for the youth than even staying astride an outlaw bronc with a burr under its saddle.

"J-Jess? Wh-What are we g-gonna do about L-Liz Anne?"

"They still got her, Dee. They got her and we'll chase 'em plum' to Jericho if we have to. Just waitin' on daylight."

"Is it wrong me th-thinkin' what I do? That I-I wanna do to them wh-what they d-done to Mr. B-Buckalew?"

"I been wonderin' the same thing, Dee."

"M-M-My ma. Sh-she was a good church-goin' p-person. Sh-She'd've said let the G-Good L-Lord handle the p-punishment."

"I expect Providence will have His say, all right," interjected Tom, "—about them butchers and what some of us have had comin' for twenty years now."

This time, Jess resisted the urge to cross-examine, but he found Tom's face by the light of the moon and saw it for what it was.

Haunted. But probably no more than Jess knew his own to be.

By daybreak, Jess had already been up for hours, watching and waiting and pondering, so he sighted the two men riding in out of the burnt orange sky while they were still distant silhouettes. He took the precaution of waking Tom and Dee, but the straight-backed, nose-in-the-air way in which one of the riders sat his horse told him it was Sorrels, and logic and a flop-eared hat dictated the identity of his companion. While they were still a couple of hundred yards away, Jess started out afoot to meet them, luring Tom and Dee along at his flank.

"Liz Anne—seen anything of Liz Anne?" he called as soon as the riders were within earshot.

While the pair was still at a distance, Gabe merely shook his head, but he answered aloud as soon as he was close enough to speak in a normal voice.

"Nothin' but dust and more dust, Jess. Just like the ol' boy ridin' drag—swallowed a bucket full to where he couldn't even make spit no more."

Jess fixed his gaze on Sorrels and kept it there as the two 7L hands rode on in and pulled rein. A rage that had been building inside Jess all through a brutal storm and troubling night reached a fever pitch as Sorrels swung down. The moment Sorrels turned, Jess met him with a two-handed push in the chest.

With a quick "What the hell?" Sorrels stumbled back against his horse.

"You could've killed her!" Jess cried. "You had to go shootin' and give 'em warnin'!"

Even in the dawn, Jess could see Sorrels burn red with a rage of his own.

"Don't blame me, you SOB," Sorrels snarled. He stepped toward him in a challenge from which Jess wouldn't back away. "All I was doin' was gettin' their range. Took a damned fool hittin' me to make me pull that trigger."

Jess wanted to tear him apart, but suddenly Gabe was between the two.

"Whoa! Ain't they enough bandidos to fight out here without you two goin' at it?"

Jess knew Gabe was right, but a part of him still

wanted nothing more than to teach Sorrels a long-overdue lesson.

"Blame yourself if you're lookin' for blame," Sorrels went on.

Jess started to spew a few invectives, but Tom cut him off with calm words of wisdom.

"I reckon," he said, "they's enough bad hombres out there to shoulder all the blame they is."

About sunrise Tom picked up a westbound trail, and Jess and his fellow 7L hands fell in behind the old cowhand. Jess could distinguish the individual tracks of five horses, but it took the stranger to point out that four sets cut deeper than the fifth. Not only that, but the spacing of the latter tracks reflected a stumbling gait, meaning that even without a rider, this animal struggled.

Jess couldn't keep from glancing back and wondering how long it would be before their own horses would cut a trace just as portentous. Still, he wished the condition of their mounts was all that troubled him.

Sorrels had fallen off the pace, prompting Jess to take his horse up abreast of Tom's so he could speak without being overheard.

"You think he's right, Tom?"

The old man only looked at him.

"Sorrels," Jess continued. "What he said about it bein' my fault he shot."

"Maybe."

Jess sighed and looked down for a moment.

"I-I'd give anything to have her back safe. If it was because of me we never got her, I . . . I don't know what I'd do."

"The same as you're doin' now, son. The best you can."

Jess studied him—the face bronzed by the sun, the crusted skin cancers, the leathery cracks at those tormented eyes.

"I get the feelin' that's not good enough for you right now, Tom."

Those burdened eyes met Jess's. "They's things we all got to do, I guess," Tom replied. "Right now we got to get that girl back."

Jess tightened his jaw and focused on the desolation ahead. "I love her. Even if she don't know it."

"Figured as much, son. Loved a girl of my own once."

Jess waited, thinking the old cowhand might have more to say. When he didn't, Jess spoke again.

"You said 'once.' Somethin' happen? Where—"

"Goin' to see her now. Soon as we're done."

As Jess turned to find the stranger's gaze searing a hole through the far-away horizon, he had plenty more to ask, but something told him this wasn't the time.

As they rode on under an increasingly brutal sun that bore down on their backs, a great thirst crawled up from Jess's throat. Only Sorrels grumbled openly; everyone else contented himself with an airtight of tomatoes. A single can made Jess only crave more, but he realized that in an oven such as this there could be only two kinds of men—smart ones and dead ones. Although he hadn't spoken to Sorrels since their confrontation, when Jess looked back and warned Dee to ration his supply, he knew that even Sorrels with that vital Winchester had gotten the message.

In mid-morning, they came upon a discarded saddle, and a few miles farther they found the dead horse that went with it. Sorrels rode on by oblivious, but Tom held his mount and called Jess's attention to the dark splotching on the roan's breast and on the nearby ground.

No one had to tell Jess why it was there. Someone had cut the horse's throat and drained its flow.

It only heightened Jess's concern for Liz Anne, for if her captors were desperate enough to drink blood, they might already have lost sight of their motive in keeping her alive in the first place.

NINE

The blood dribbling down the Mexicans' chins made them seem all the more evil.

From her position in the saddle, Liz Anne watched the riders pass the boot, the second time they had slaked their thirst since the shrivel-armed man had drawn a knife across the horse's throat back up-trail. Prior to that, as long ago as the subsiding of the storm, they had pushed on into the night, and the coming of day had found them in a gray wasteland. Now, a killer sun held them in its power, and Liz Anne prayed that it would claim her quickly.

She had been determined not to drink when they had first caught the boot full, but the three of them had held her and forced the thick, hot liquid down her throat. Against her wishes the blood had rallied her a little, even as it had nauseated, but now she had ceased to sweat again. Thanks to her father, she recognized it as an early symptom of heat exhaustion, which if not arrested could advance to stroke and death. If she could only deny their attempts to force her to drink again, she might soon achieve the only escape possible.

But now the three of them were upon her again, one holding her horse, another prying open her jaws, the third pouring the blood down between her teeth. With hands tied to the saddle horn, she had no choice but to try to drown herself.

That is, if she only knew how. The truth was, she was helpless to do anything but gag and gurgle as the blood filled her throat and revived her again.

As they rode on, she wiped her mouth against her shoulder and tried for the first time to engage any of them in conversation.

"How . . . How come you doin' this?" she asked the shrivel-armed man who rode abreast.

"Dinero. Mucho dinero."

"Wasn't ten dollars at the ranch."

"Mucho across the Bravo."

"Mexico? What's there?"

"Rich patron," said the capitan. "Pay bueno for white girl."

"Th-That's what all this is about? That's why you killed . . ."

She couldn't bring herself to say the words, or even broach the violation of her body. But she had no trouble voicing a great truth.

"I'll die first—I swear I will."

A vicious scowl swept over the Mexican's face. "No! I'll get mucho dinero and they'll know Perez as a great patron someday!"

Seeing Perez's eyes narrow and the veins bulge at his temples, Liz Anne sensed that her best hope might be to bait him into killing her.

"No," she told him. "They'll just know you as a coward for what you did."

Almost before she realized it, Perez had cut his mount against hers and brought a knife flashing up to her throat. The blade was stained dark, as it had been ever since he had similarly lifted it against her father.

It was the last image Liz Anne carried with her as she closed her eyes.

"Do it," she said. "Do it, you coward."

She felt the blade tighten against her larynx and anticipated the quick slice that would open her up just like that horse.

"Dinero, Perez! You forget the money!"

The cry was in Spanish, but with the working knowledge of the language she had gained from her father, Liz Anne understood the guttural of the scar-faced Mexican the others called Rodriquez. Nor was the ensuing exchange between Perez and one-eyed Ernesto any less clear.

"Let me have her!" Ernesto pleaded.

"Shut up!"

"Let me! Then you can kill her!"

Suddenly the pressure against Liz Anne's throat eased, and she opened her eyes to find Perez sheathing the blade and whipping out a revolver.

"It's me that's capitan—not either one of you cabrons!" He swung the muzzle up against Liz Anne's temple. "It's me that says if she lives or dies!"

"Do it," Liz Anne said again. "Just do it, you coward."

She closed her eyes once more and felt the muzzle tremble against her hairline as if in the grip of a man grappling with rage. Then the naked steel was gone, and she reeled to a sudden blow to her mouth.

Her horse shied, and she fell to one side as far as her secured hands would allow. She looked up, seeing little specks dance between her and Perez.

"It's me that says!" he cried. "Nobody else!"

With or without Perez's help, Liz Anne didn't think her hours on earth would be long. "The easiest thing to do is die," her father had told her once. "The hard part is living."

If anybody had known, it would have been her father, who had come so close to losing his will to live after the Apaches had raided on that long-ago morning. Day after day, Liz Anne had found him standing at the little mound of rocks as dust had powdered his boots. Yet somehow he had overcome—by the grace of the Good Lord, he had said. But with the travails that these indescribable vermin had cast upon Liz Anne, she felt that God not only had forsaken her, but had cast all the dark forces of nature against her.

For a while, she had worn a dead man's hat, until the devil storm had swept it away. Now her eyes were bared against torturous rays. Her face burned with an inner fire that heightened by the minute. Her cracked lips felt as swollen as her tongue, and every time she turned her head, the world spun ever so slightly.

Death under the sun might not have been her preference, but at least it was doing its job with certainty.

Liz Anne's greatest regret in surrendering her life was losing what might have been with Jess. Their budding relationship offered so much promise, but she had scarcely paid him any mind when he had first ridden for the 7Ls the previous summer. Of course, she had been only a girl then, but another year at the boarding school in San Angelo had matured her in so many ways.

When she had come out to the ranch at Christmas, she still had barely known his name, but by the time classes had resumed it had been Jess, of all the hands, who had earned a place in her dreams. Every time he had come to the house to confer with her father, she had casually sauntered in—always, of course, without seeming forward, for that would have been construed as less than lady-like. Jess had always seemed a little tongue-tied, though, and had never mumbled more than a polite greeting.

All of that had changed, however, when Liz Anne's father had dispatched Jess to San Angelo with the buckboard to bring Liz Anne home at the end of the spring term. It was a two-day trip, and Jess treated her like royalty all through the first morning. Polite to a fault, he seemed too intimidated even to make conversation.

But when they camped on the Concho in late afternoon, she became determined to get him to smile. The moment finally came as they sat at river's edge; she splashed him with water and he splashed back, and both of them giggled like kids. All the way on to the 7Ls, they talked incessantly and with such obviously mutual enjoyment that Liz Anne actually hated to see the ranch come into view.

On into early summer, Jess clearly concocted excuses to drop by headquarters on supposed ranch business. Even Liz Anne's father saw through the pretense, for when Jess had ridden away one evening and her father turned with a shake of his head at the trivial nature of Jess's visit, he saw her cast eyes after Jess and finally understood.

Liz Anne had worried that her father might not approve; after all, he had come from a respected Virginia family while Jess was just an uneducated cowhand. But the gleam in her eye must have been difficult to disguise, and her father had set her at ease with a simple remark that had spoken volumes.

"You could do worse."

But now so very much had changed. Neither Jess nor any other man would ever want her after what these offspring of Satan had taken from her. And even though she knew it was wrong, Liz Anne beseeched God to strike her dead.

Crack!

A stupendous explosion dropped her horse to its knees, throwing her forward across the animal's neck. Tied to the horn, she had no choice but to hang on. The bay was up quickly, wobbly as a newly foaled colt, but Rodriquez and Ernesto had not fared as well—the lightning bolt had felled their horses and rolled the men across cacti and rocks.

"*Madre de Dios!*"

Perez's horse alone kept its legs beneath it, even as it staggered to the Mexican's cry.

Liz Anne looked at the sky. She had been so caught up in reverie that she had failed to notice the angry mass that had billowed up out of the southwest. Boiling with whorls of alkali-colored sand, it would have looked little different from the storm of the previous day if not for one chilling detail that identified its origin as a special pit in hell.

The cloud was alive with sky fire, a thousand spidery fingers pulsating behind a transparent veil.

Liz Anne's ears were still ringing when the sun disappeared. Not a drop of rain ensued, but the lightning continued to pop all about, torching a nearby yucca, splintering rock, gouging holes. At the very moment that she accepted it all as a prayer answered, Jess's name played on her lips. A part of her wanted to die, all right, but the memory of his face nevertheless infused her with at least a measure of hope.

"*Maria purisima!*"

To Perez's cry and a kick of his boot, his horse bolted and the tow rope snapped taut, dragging Liz Anne's mount forward. But both horses were still dazed, and although the thunder terrified the animals, they could do little more than stumble a few yards and stop.

There, in the face of an electrical storm beyond anything Liz Anne had ever imagined, the two ponies sheltered their heads between their knees and emitted the most mournful, frightened moans she had ever heard. She knew that animals could sense things beyond the ken of man, but she didn't need any help recognizing the end of the world. Hunched over the saddle horn, Liz Anne could only welcome it, but as she sat erect to make herself a better target for the final strike, she saw something so macabre that it gave her pause.

An eery greenish fog rose up ahead and swept straight toward her. It churned across the wasteland, a glowing cloud at ground level that devoured yucca and bear grass, tasajillo and mesquite—everything that dared stay in its path.

Shaken, Liz Anne could only stare in awe and await its coming. An odor like burning sulphur singed her nostrils, and then the fog was upon her, reaching out like a living thing to seize her. Enveloping her horse's ears and racing down its neck, the glow split at the saddle horn and fell away on either side.

Liz Anne traced its path, left and right, and found tongues of flame at her boots. They shone as red as the tips of the bay's ears, yet she felt nothing but a chilling fear.

Checking, she found the same uncanny discharge on Perez's horse, while his lieutenants on the ground reached for their reins with fingers similarly lighted by fire. It would have been enough to raise the hair of the toughest cowhand, but for Liz Anne it was all just another taste of the hell she had endured ever since the Mexicans had stormed the house in the black of night.

Another devastating blast rocked the land, this one so near that Liz Anne felt as if a thousand needles struck her. The uncomfortable tingling persisted as a knife slashed her bonds and rough hands dragged her from the saddle. Suddenly the ground surged upward, crushing her shoulder. Then Perez's face was in hers as they sprawled at the hoofs of horses too stunned to break free of the Mexican's hold on reins and rope.

Liz Anne realized that the Mexican sought to save them from lightning strike, but Perez's efforts didn't end with the two of them sprawled flat. Witch fire played along his revolver barrel, and with another oath he flung the weapon into the fog.

The nearer horse shied, and between the frame of its forelegs Liz Anne saw the six-shooter come to rest a dozen or so yards away. There, glinting in the flashing lightning, it tempted—a quick and certain end to all of Liz Anne's horrors if she could only reach it.

Her chance came when the foul-breathed man cried out and unburdened her of his weight. Liz Anne didn't understand his frantic retreat, but that didn't keep her from scrambling to her hands and knees. Just as she gained her feet, she saw what terrified Perez so. From the electrically charged fog sixty yards beyond the revolver loomed a ball of lightning—there was no other way to describe it—and the glowing mass hugged the turf as it rolled toward her like a fiery barrel.

Maybe she could have held her ground and assured her end, or maybe not, but Liz Anne wouldn't leave anything to fortune. She bolted for the six-shooter, her every step carrying her closer to that oncoming sphere.

She measured time against distance and prayed that whatever the outcome, it would reunite her with her father. But at the same time, the memory of Jess wouldn't go away. If . . . If . . . If—the word haunted her even as she neared the only peace she could imagine any more.

Liz Anne reached the revolver a split second ahead of the luminous ball and lunged for the grip. Then the brightness was upon her, crackling and blinding a mere instant before it exploded in her ears.

She must have blacked out, for the next thing she knew, her cheek was against alkali and there was a sharp pain in her pelvic bone. She was awake but she was asleep, and she seemed to have a shadow self that felt and saw and heard for her. It listened to the rapid-fire thunder, watched her roll to her side, felt her grope for the revolver pinned against her pelvis by her fall.

Liz Anne's shadow self alone was aware as her hand closed on the weapon and her index finger slipped through the trigger guard. The six-shooter's weight was surprising, even daunting, and she found herself lifting it with both hands. Even then it was unsteady, but her disassociated twin managed to cock the hammer.

In Liz Anne's dream world, she saw herself achieve a sitting position and look past her upraised knee at a charging Perez. He was only strides away, his sweat-beaded face wrenched by exertion as he spewed a stream of profanity.

Here was the man who had robbed her of so much—not only her past, lost in her father's blood, but her very future. Perez was evil incarnate and he would live on, doing harm wherever he went while her father rotted in his grave and the children she had long held in her heart never found rest in her arms. She had time for but a single bullet, one either to spare herself from a far worse destiny, or to spare so many others of the foulest maggot the world had ever known.

At point-blank range, Liz Anne's shadow self squeezed the trigger.

TEN

Even that twenty-year-old trail to the Pecos, for all the horrors it brought in the end, had not portended as ominous as this.

The foxfire was all around Tom, ghostly auras that outlined his pony's ears, hugged his spur rowels, clung to the hat brims of his fellow riders. It floated blue and silver and red, forming cones about his fingers as sky fire raged and a greenish fog of electricity settled over them with a smell like burning sulphur.

"All over our guns!" exclaimed Sorrels. "Gotta get rid of 'em!"

Tom saw the 7L hand reaching for his glowing Winchester. "Keep 'em holstered!" he shouted in competition with the lightning's *pop! pop! pop!* "You're dead without 'em anyways, soon's we catch up with them killers!"

Concentrated hell bombed the nearby flats, and the lightning-rent sky answered with a crash like the collective cries of the damned. Not even on his drives to Kansas had Tom experienced such an electrical storm, but he had seen firsthand what lightning could do to a man.

Just north of the Big Red one night, a bolt had struck a South Texas drover doing his best to hold a boogered herd. Tom and a couple of hands had ridden upon the grisly scene at daybreak, their stomachs heaving to the awful stench of charred flesh. The strike had set the man's shirt afire and melted his pocket watch, but that wasn't the half of it. Blasting his hat into a hundred shreds, the bolt had split his head so deeply that his face was no longer recognizable.

"It g-gonna get us, J-Jess? It gonna g-get us?" asked Dee.

"Sittin' tall like prairie dogs outa their hole!" said Gabe.

"Get off of these horses!"

The cry came from Jess, enough reason for Sorrels to take time to comment. "What I been tellin' you!"

But Tom had already dismounted without prompting, more than foxfire going with him. He couldn't shed the memory of riding back to a little hard-scrabble homestead in South Texas and facing a haggard woman with three dirty-faced kids with the news that her husband would never be coming home.

Tom spun, searching as the 7L riders stepped off and clung to reins as they took cover under their animals.

"No good, son!" he yelled to Jess. "Get away from 'em! Get away!"

A dozen yards distant, the ghost fires danced on a catclaw bush, the only nearby vegetation of significant size.

"There!" rasped Tom.

As fast as his bum leg would allow, he dragged his skittish horse over and secured the reins with a quick half-hitch around the shrub's stem. The others followed suit, Tom reaching in to help Dee after Sorrels bumped the young hand in his haste. Maybe it hadn't been deliberate, but Tom fumed at how Sorrels just stood in the way, cursing those clawing limbs that had gashed his hand.

Securing the second pony, Tom grabbed Dee by the arm. "This a-way!"

He pulled the boy with him as he tried to distance himself from the horses as quickly as possible. Suddenly the sky seemed to split all the way to the sun, everything flashing white as something cut Tom's legs out from under him. He was already down before the jarring volts and deafening *crack!* registered on his senses, but there was nothing subtle about the spasms in his legs and twitch in his fingers, or about his abrupt difficulty finding a breath.

"T-Tom! M-Mister Tom! You okay, M-Mister Tom?"

In a detached sort of way, Tom knew that somebody was talking to him, just as he knew that a hand was shaking his shoulder.

"Stay down, Dee! Stay down! You—" Jess's voice also drifted through Tom's semi-consciousness, the blaring thunder cutting his words short.

"We gonna d-die, M-Mister Tom? W-We gonna d-die?"

As soon as Tom could get air in his lungs, his head began to clear and all the twitching started to subside. He rolled to his side, finding Dee sprawled next to him, his pimply face buried under a hat two sizes too big. The teenager's every panicky word seemed strangely muffled, but the high-pitched hum in Tom's shell-shocked ears was all too clear.

"W-We gonna d-die, ain't we? M-Mister Tom, we—"

Tom stretched out a hand and found Dee's shoulder. "Gonna be all right, young fellow. Just tough it out—gonna be fine."

When Dee peeked out from under his hat, Tom saw an ashen face accentuated by wide, terrified eyes.

"Y-You ever pr-pray, M-Mister Tom? M-My ma, sh-she always said I oughta pray wh-when it come up a st-storm."

Tom had prayed, all right, but not since those adobe walls on the Pecos when he had cried out again and again for help that had come too late for Sarah. Having ridden for nature's brand from the time he had been old enough to fork a horse, he had a profound respect for the forces that shaped every single day. Still, for twenty years now, he had struggled through each waking hour knowing that the Creator must not give a hang about him or Sarah or anybody else.

But that didn't keep Dee from keeping up his desperate plea that one of them should call upon the Almighty.

"Might listen better from you, young fellow," Tom told him. "You just go on and pray for the both of us."

Dee did just that, not only beseeching God to set His angels charge over all of them, but asking that blessings rain down on Tom in particular. No matter Dee's stuttering, Tom had never heard a more fervent and heartfelt prayer, and he couldn't help but be moved by the way this backward kid had singled him out. But Tom was no less struck by the youngster's conviction that God actually cared, and he suddenly wished that he could have that same sort of assurance.

For relentless minutes the storm held Tom and the others at its mercy, the dry lightning sparing them even as it unleashed its fury on surrounding yucca and scrub mesquite. Almost as important, the horses eluded strike after strike, but they kept up a constant moaning that raised the hair on Tom's neck. Facing away from the animals, he was too busy keeping his cheek against alkali to risk a glance back until the lightning suddenly abated and a pony squealed in pain.

Turning, Tom saw a coyote dodge a vicious hoof. Almost simultaneously, a second canine darted in, nipping the appaloosa's already bloody hock.

"Eatin' 'em alive!" he exclaimed.

The stirring horses fought to break free, but the catclaw held fast as the coyotes concentrated on the appaloosa. The pony's next kick landed flush, rolling one of the coyotes, but the canine was up instantly to resume the attack. The two seemed to work as a team, one distracting the horse while the second rushed its flank.

Suddenly a revolver boomed three times in quick succession, followed by the blast of a shotgun. Twisting around to the 7L hands who sprawled twenty feet away, Tom saw Jess's arm recoiling from yet another shot while the barrel of Gabe's twelve gauge swung with the flight of the coyotes.

"Go savin' on your powder!" Tom shouted. "They ain't—"

"Th-Th-They's right on t-t-top of us!"

Tom rolled over at Dee's cry, finding a tawny hide and bared fangs almost in his face. All he had time to do was throw out an arm and seize a white-furred throat, but four feet and forty pounds of determined coyote were nevertheless upon him. He could see the black-tipped guard hairs across its shoulders and the one-inch spacing between the stiletto-like teeth, but mostly he saw those eyes— dark orbs at once both cunning and possessed.

Just as he fended off the first strike, he realized he was in even greater trouble. Another set of fangs swept across his vision, and suddenly there was a second set of reddish-brown forelegs pressing the attack.

Years before, Tom had seen a couple of coyotes work in tandem to hamstring a yearling steer and suffocate it with a choke hold, but he had never known one to pounce on a man. Maybe his prone position made him appear crippled or weak, or perhaps the attack reflected desperation in a drouth-ravaged land stripped of prey. Later on he could ponder the matter, but he would never get the chance unless he fought off these hellhounds that seemed determined to tear him apart.

Just as things seemed grimmest, while jaws snapped like steel traps and a blur of fur revealed sky only in glimpses, a third form entered the fray with a cry. Arms other than Tom's flailed wildly, seizing hides and casting them aside in mad frenzy, and suddenly Tom was free.

He rolled away, hearing abrupt screams of agony, then started at the powerful discharge of a revolver close at hand.

"Git outa here! Git! Git!"

He looked up and found Jess hurdling his legs, the cowhand's six-shooter and senses fixed on something beyond. Tom whirled with Jess's course to see his .41 recoil, then the coyotes vanished into the desert and Jess dropped to a writhing Dee a half-dozen feet from Tom.

Not since the Comanches had carved up those screaming teamsters at Horsehead Crossing had

Tom seen so much blood on a living person. The skin at Dee's neck was all mangled, shreds of flesh dripping red, and there were terrible puncture wounds on his cheek, above his eye, all over his hands.

"Good Lord, Dee. Good Lord. Good Lord."

A white-faced Jess seemed at a loss for what to do except mutter and place a caring hand on the tossing youngster's shoulder. Then Gabe was there too, kneeling alongside the wagon boss, his fingers frantically working a bandana free from his own neck.

"Gotta stop the bleedin', Jess," Gabe said. "Got to quick."

Jess turned, the shock still in his face, but he took the bandana as Gabe stuffed it in his hand.

"Gonna be all right, Dee," Jess told the young hand. "Just lay still."

But the boy moaned and thrashed in such pain and fright that Jess couldn't apply direct pressure where it was needed most.

"You gotta stop movin', Dee," pleaded Jess. "My Lord, you gotta stop, you gotta stop."

As Tom struggled to his feet, he saw Gabe grip the boy's shoulders and steady him against the ground.

"I ever tell you," Gabe asked Dee, " 'bout the time an ol' bronc throwed me right a-straddle a fence?"

But the blood kept coming, turning the wadded

bandana dark as Jess pressed it against Dee's throat.

"Might as well leave him alone. Be slobberin' at the mouth come mornin'."

Tom whirled. At his shoulder, Sorrels stood watching the desperate scene.

"Rabid coyote bite you that a-way," Sorrels went on, "you're already good as dead."

With a cross-body sweep of his hand, Tom seized his single-action revolver and brought the muzzle flashing up between Sorrels's eyes. Tom saw him go ashen as fear flooded that angular face.

Gripped by a rage he hadn't known in twenty years, Tom thumbed back the hammer.

"I ain't never shot a man in cold blood, but so help me God you say another word and I'll do it!"

Tom knew he had put the fear of the Almighty in him, for he could see it in Sorrels's eyes and hear him search for a breath that wasn't there. For second after tense second, Tom kept that muzzle in place, his finger quaking against trigger. Dee had dived in to save his life at terrible cost, and this bastard in front of him had the disrespect to add to the poor kid's terror. The SOB! He'd put a pistol ball right through his damned—

"Tom. Tom."

Jess's quiet voice broke the wall of Tom's rage.

"Tom. Need your help, Tom."

121

For another moment the revolver trembled in Tom's hands as he held his stare, then with an oath he withdrew the barrel and eased the hammer into place.

As Sorrels fell away, gasping for air, Tom turned and found Jess and Gabe looking at him.

"It's all right, Tom," said Jess. "Come here."

Tom had a hard time drawing a breath of his own, but he holstered his weapon and went to Dee. He knelt before him, struck by the degree of fear in the boy's mauled face. When Tom had confronted Sorrels, he had been in control of things, but now he just felt utterly helpless.

He tore a strip from his own shirttail and dabbed the oozing puncture wounds about Dee's eye. "The thing you done," he told him, "you ain't got no idea how much it means to me."

Dee turned those terrified eyes to him and clutched his arm with a bloody hand. "Th-Th-Them wolves m-m-mad, M-Mister Tom? Th-Them wolves m-m-mad?"

For a moment, Tom wished he had pulled that trigger. "You listen to me, young fellow. I seen them things eyeball to eyeball. They was sure 'nough hungry and plenty desperate, but they wasn't neither one of 'em had hydrophoby."

"B-But S-Sorrels—"

"The hell with Sorrels," said Jess. "What he don't know would make a book so big you couldn't lift it with a block and tackle."

"Yeah," said Gabe, forcing a grin. "He's the yay-hoo that told me that bronc wouldn't pitch a lick. Next thing I knowed I was ridin' that fence and singin' in a high voice."

As the three of them continued to reassure, Dee began to calm enough for Tom to assess the severity of his wounds. His hands were all chewed, and the puncture marks on his face went clear to the bone, the eye socket alone sparing Dee's vision. His throat was the worst, but as Jess stifled the bleeding and momentarily withdrew the soaked bandana, Tom was relieved to see that the bites had missed the carotid artery. Although the skin looked as if it has passed through a meat grinder, the wound seemed relatively superficial for the amount of blood.

The boy had been lucky, but with a pang of guilt, Tom could only imagine the kind of pain and emotional trauma he faced. Even more worrisome was the prospect of what those bacteria-laden bites might wreak in the way of infection—hydrophobia or no hydrophobia.

A half-hour later, with the overcast sky less volatile and Dee's bleeding subsiding, Tom knew it was time for them to reach a decision. He considered their options as he tore strips from a dingy shirt out of his war bag, and continued to dwell on the matter as Jess bandaged Dee's neck, forehead, and hands. With dehydration a concern, he helped sit the boy up and started him on their last airtight of tomatoes, then Jess stepped away and motioned with his head.

Tom followed, and so did Gabe, and when they were all out of earshot, Jess stopped and the three huddled on skeleton plain.

The color was still gone from Jess's face. "What are we gonna do? In God's name, what we gonna do? Liz Anne's still out there and Dee's all chewed up."

"Bleedin's about quit, but that ain't the half of it, Jess," said Gabe, his characteristic grin only a memory. "That sun pops out and it can finish what them howlers started."

Jess looked down and shook his head. "Somebody tell me what to do. Somebody tell me."

Tom cleared the alkali dust out of his throat. "Expect we's as close to the Pecos now as the Concho. That boy's gotta have water, son, but he needs mendin' just as bad. They's a settlement, Stockton, a hard day's ride past Horsehead. If we can't get him doctored there, we can wagon him on north to the Texas Pacific."

Jess lifted his troubled gaze. "That's where those Mexicans seem headed, don't they? Horsehead Crossin'? You sayin' we can keep on their trail without hurtin' Dee?"

One glance at Dee was enough to assail Tom with doubts. "I don't figure it matters much. He's as bad off headin' one way as he is the other."

Jess cast questioning eyes on Gabe.

"One thing's for sure, Jess," Gabe said in response. "Can't just shut her down here and expect Dee to make it. None of the rest of us either."

Jess turned toward Dee, and as Tom studied the profile of the 7L boss's pale features, he truly felt for him. Dee, Tom had known only a couple of days, but the lost waif had already earned a place deep in Tom's rough-hewn heart. Jess, meanwhile, had helped look after the kid for who-knew-how-long now, and Tom could only imagine his whirlwind of emotions in this dilemma.

The young fellow or that girl.

That girl or the young fellow.

It was Jess who broke a long silence, even as he continued to stare at Dee.

"I hope we ain't wrong doin' this, Gabe. I . . ." His voice cracked and he turned. "I hope the Good Lord forgives us if we are, Tom. Let's get Dee in the saddle and gain some on those murderin' whoresons before dark."

The sky mercifully stayed overcast as their horses crept on, living skeletons destined to become dead ones if they didn't find water soon. Puffs of dust rose from every hoof and settled in Tom's throat, but he could no longer muster enough saliva to wash it down. He tried sucking on a pebble to stimulate a little spit, but his mouth continued so dry that he had to use his fingers to pry the rock from his tongue.

There were even more troubling signs. Although he had managed to urinate before mounting up, the result had been only a dark and foul dribble. Too, as he examined his hands, he saw folds of skin across the knuckles, more evidence of a body crying out for water.

As much as Tom suffered, though, he knew it was far worse for Dee. The youth slumped over the horn, his crude bandages a red flag of distress. He seemed dazed, as much from dehydration as his wounds, and Tom worried that he might tumble from the saddle. No matter from whose perspective Tom considered things, there was no denying a terrible truth.

None of them—neither man nor animal—was likely to survive another day in the sun without drink.

ELEVEN

Dusk found Tom at a place that stirred memories forgotten for two decades. There was nothing remarkable about the flanking ridges, gray in barrenness, or about the bottomland unfurling sterile except for eight-foot yucca and pint-sized mesquites. But as his appaloosa plodded along, obliterating the very tracks they chased, he noticed a sculpted dirt butte near ground level fifty yards to his right. He couldn't see much from his vantage point, but the suggestion of erosion and an abrupt sense of familiarity led him to turn his horse off-trail.

"What is it, Tom?"

He had no answer for Jess until he pulled rein where the land fell away ten or twelve feet to a limestone bed with a crazy-quilt of shallow catchment basins. The depression was as dry as his throat, the rock pockets cradling only crusty earth, but a profusion of deeply gouged tracks told of onetime mud.

On that long-ago day they had paused at this very spot, he and Sarah and all the rest, to lament a water hole just as dry and no less trampled by mustangs. He knew that it was a thirsty horse's instinct to paw at dry earth to create seepage; even on this elevated bank his appaloosa was doing such this very moment. What might still lie hidden in those dirt-filled basins?

His face was solely on those *tinajas* as he dismounted and tied his reins to a scrub mesquite. He started down the bank, not realizing how weak he was until his boot slipped in the rubble and he didn't have the strength to keep his legs under him. Landing on his hip, he did a controlled slide the rest of the way down and stumbled over to a rock pocket at the sink's low point.

He reached for the pocketknife with which he had castrated so many calves, then eased to his knees. They burned with an inner fire, but that was the least of his worries as he began to dig.

Tom glimpsed movement nearby, and he looked up to see Jess drop before an adjacent tinaja, a knife of his own in his hand. Then Sorrels was close by as well, digging with a frenzy, and Tom glanced toward the bank and saw Gabe helping Dee off his horse.

Tom dug, and dug deeper, scraping out with fingernails what he loosened. He struck underlying rock without finding even a hint of moisture, then started in on another tinaja. The three of them—four, once Gabe set to work—must have looked like prairie dogs, he figured, the way they littered that depression with holes. But try as Tom might, the soil persisted as dry as adobe dust.

Tom was the first to stand and close his knife. Then Jess and Gabe were on their feet too, leaving Sorrels grunting and wheezing as he continued to dig obsessively. For a full minute, there were only the scrape of Sorrels's blade and patter of flying dirt as Tom and the others looked on.

"No use, Sorrels," Jess finally said.

Tom let out a sigh of resignation and looked toward the swirls of brightness low in the fading western sky.

Sorrels cursed. "Shouldn't have ever wasted our last airtight on that kid! He ain't—"

Tom spun, his anger flaring. He saw Sorrels cast a quick look in his direction, but the moment their gazes locked, the 7L hand went pale and lowered his head.

Tom almost wished that Sorrels hadn't caught himself, for he felt so utterly helpless again that he lamented once more not putting a bullet in him. But he had greater concerns for now, for he could read crushing despair on everyone's face. Tom, too, already had a foot in the grave, and he realized he was sinking deeper by the moment.

"What are we gonna do, Jess?" asked a gravelly voiced Gabe. "What in Sam Hill we gonna do?"

Without looking up, the 7L boss bit his lip. "Liz Anne—I ain't leavin' her, Gabe. I can't." He lifted his eyes. "For Dee's sake, Tom, you sure we're closer to the Pecos?"

"If we wasn't before, sure 'nough are now."

Sorrels had approached Jess from behind, and now he seized his shoulder and whirled him about.

"We're gonna die out here, you SOB!" he cried. "Coulda got you a growed woman, but you gotta drag us after some little whore that—"

Jess swung from the hip and clipped Sorrels on the jaw with enough force to stagger him. Sorrels reeled back and sank to both knees. He knelt there, shaking his downed head in an obvious daze, but Jess lunged after him to finish what he had started.

"I shoulda let Tom kill you! You—"

Tom clutched Jess's arm in mid-swing. "Easy, son," he said as Jess spun with fire in his eyes.

"Save what strength you got, 'cause we gotta ride—and keep a-ridin' till we find water."

Night brought a gloom more ominous than anything Tom had faced since the siege at Horsehead. They rode, trusting their horse's instincts and night vision to trace the beaten road. About midnight, Tom got off his appaloosa and struck a match on his boot sole to reassure himself. He had to kneel and shade his eyes against the glare, but he managed to discern recent horse tracks threading onward.

When he planted a foot back in the stirrup, he rocked a dozen times before realizing he just didn't have the strength to climb back on. But he kept trying, too proud to ask for help, though not too proud to accept it when Jess dismounted and boosted him up in the saddle.

As the night wore on, Tom no longer seemed to be astride a horse. He was walking beside a creaking wagon, reins in hand as he periodically called out "Gee!" or "Haw!" to a team of plodding oxen that kicked up dust. Sarah was beside him, the alkali collecting on her dress as she trudged without complaint, even though the birth of their first child was only months away. By then, Tom anticipated, a Texas crippled by Reconstruction would be far behind, and he would have already set up a tent along some rippling stream in the promising West. Before the winter snows, he would have a roof over their heads and enough wood to stoke the fireplace until spring. The cabin would be modest, just a single room, but he could always add to it to accommodate the patter of more small feet as the Good Lord saw fit.

It would constitute a shelter, all right, but most of all it would be a home, filled not only with love, but with hope for tomorrow.

The rattle of a saddle and a loud thud shook Tom back to the hopelessness of the here and now.

"Dee's horse is down!" shouted Jess.

Wheeling his mount, Tom saw for himself. Two dark forms, a large and a small, sprawled on the ground, and one was as still as the other. Jess and Gabe were already stepping off, something that Tom couldn't afford to do.

"Young fellow all right?" he asked as they dropped to Dee's side. "Horse plum' died on its feet!"

"Out cold!" Jess's voice was as hoarse as Tom's. "But I can still feel him breathin' against my hand!"

"Loosen his belt, son. Fan him in the face with your hat."

Jess and Gabe did exactly that, but for minute after troubling minute Tom detected no change in the shadowy scene. Still, low to the ground, the vague outline of a hat kept moving back and forth to Jess's constant "Come on, Dee, come on," the only other thing the 7L wagon boss could do.

The situation couldn't have looked grimmer,

and again Tom felt all kinds of regret. Had it been within his power, he would have traded places with Dee and considered it small payment. Maybe Tom didn't have it in his make-up to gush emotionally over an act of kindness, but he would never forget the kid's sacrifice on his behalf.

"Young fellow's one to pray quite a bit," Tom said, surprising even himself. "Maybe one of you can—"

"He's comin' around!" exclaimed Jess.

Sure enough, Dee was stirring a little and beginning to moan.

"Right here, Dee," said Jess. "Me and Gabe both."

"Th-th-thirsty. S-So th-th-th-thirsty."

"I know, I know. We're headed for water. Gotta get you on a horse."

But as Jess and Gabe tried to sit him up, Dee again lost consciousness and went limp.

"No way he's ever gonna ride, Jess," said Gabe.

"I don't think it's the fall as much as ever'thing else," said Jess. "Maybe if we just keep on fannin'."

"Enough, damn it! Enough!"

Apart from the group, Sorrels had sat in disinterested silence until now.

"I ain't waitin' another minute on that kid!" he continued as he rose. "Go ahead and shoot me, you SOBs! We're dead anyway soon's that sun comes up!"

This time, Tom knew Sorrels was right. Already,

the moon was beginning to break through the haze, and sunup would catch them in a forge that would seal their doom.

"Dee . . . Dee," persisted Jess in his efforts to bring the youth around.

"Just ain't gonna work, Jess," said Gabe.

Tom would make it work. "You boys do me a favor. Lift the young fellow up astride my horse in front of me here."

"I can take him on mine, Tom," said Jess.

Tom took his mount closer. "Expect I'm slighter than any of you. Be less a burden on my horse. Here, let me have him."

They pushed on relentlessly, trying to wrench as many miles out of the night as they could. But their horses were spent, and the night had only so many hours.

With the approach of daylight, Tom finally admitted to himself the inevitable. He couldn't keep that sun from coming up, he couldn't drag that river any closer, and he couldn't afford to coax his appaloosa into more than a labored walk. Even as it was, he expected the poor animal to pitch forward and die at any moment.

Water was still as distant as that low-hanging moon ahead, and all Tom could do was let what-was-going-to-happen happen.

Unless . . .

To what lengths would desperation drive a man

in order to survive? Would he do the unthinkable, the unimaginable? Just minutes ago, Sorrels had wished aloud that he had tapped a vein in the dead horse. Had Tom had his wits, he would have bled the carcass himself. Second-guessing was useless, but Sorrels's lament had started Tom to thinking. If one of them had to die to give the other four a chance, there wasn't a doubt in his mind who that person should be.

Tom glanced back at Sorrels in the moonlight, measuring him for a sunrise pistol ball.

Morning broke with a gloom that belied a white-hot sun on fire in a sky that seemed never to have seen a cloud. They were on an elevated tableland, a southern neck of the Staked Plains, and a vast funeral procession of many-daggered yucca and bear grass tufts stretched to a distant range, flat-topped and gray across the western horizon. Tom recognized the sweeping ridge as the Castle Mountains, a marker to the Pecos a scant thirteen miles beyond. But he also recognized a ride of another day or day and a half, a demand the five of them just couldn't meet.

All through the arduous night, Tom had felt Dee's blood hot and wet against his supporting arm. It had been the only thing that had told him the boy was still alive. But now daylight revealed a limp form pale as death, his head slumped to the side to expose a bandaged throat dark and portentous.

The only saving grace, thought Tom, was that unconsciousness mercifully spared the kid the realization that sunup had caught them so many terrible miles from water and hope.

It was time, and Tom knew it. He pulled rein, and the other riders stopped with him. He tried to speak, but the dry alkali loomed too thick in his throat.

Jess coughed, as if clearing dust from his own voice. "Tom?"

Tom could manage only a hoarse whisper as he nodded to Dee. "Slide him off for me."

Jess and Gabe relieved Tom of his burden and stretched the moaning youth out in the elongated shade of a yucca. Sorrels, too, dismounted to collapse under a yucca nearer the sunrise. But Tom stayed frozen to the saddle, his right leg unresponsive as he willed it to swing across the appaloosa's withers.

Tom looked at Jess bending over Dee, and Jess looked back. Then the 7L boss came around the appaloosa, took the reins without comment, and slipped Tom's boot from the stirrup. As soon as Jess lifted the numb leg up and over, Tom succeeded in sliding off. Still, he had to support himself with the horn before enough feeling returned for him to stumble toward Sorrels.

Sorrels had dragged himself up to a sitting position, but his eyes were closed as his head slumped against the yucca's stem. Tom's arm, having clutched Dee for so long, was almost as dead as his leg as he reached cross-body for his revolver, but he knew what to do when he pulled it out. Hovering over the unaware man, he drew back the hammer with an ominous click that opened Sorrels's eyes into the muzzle of that eight-inch barrel.

"Tom?" Jess's concerned voice rose up from off to his right. "What are you about to do, Tom?"

"Weakest horse," he half-whispered. "Cut its throat."

"What do you—"

"Won't be needin' it. Take your boot, bleed it out."

"For God's sake!" cried Sorrels.

"Doin' you a favor," rasped Tom. "Oughta just leave you."

Out of the corner of his eye, Tom saw Jess slowly approach. He was equally aware when Jess pulled his .41 and hesitantly lifted it, but even as Tom heard him cock the weapon, his focus stayed on Sorrels's terrified eyes.

"I . . ." Jess's quaking voice had all kinds of reluctance. "I can't let you do this, Tom."

Still, Tom didn't flinch. "Young fellow's dyin'. Devils has got that girl. You can, 'cause you got to."

Jess went silent, and the suspense mounted with every twitch of Sorrels's ashen cheek.

"Kill him!" Sorrels begged. "Good God, kill him! Kill him!"

With peripheral vision, Tom saw Jess's .41 slowly drop.

"It's all right, son," said Tom, still staring at Sorrels over the gun barrel. "You got to hurry."

Jess hesitated. "Tom—"

"Just don't look this way no more."

Tom never turned, but he was aware as Jess slunk away, just as he knew when Gabe staggered after him to the appaloosa. In the same way, Tom's senses told him when Jess snubbed the animal against a stout yucca and unfolded his pocketknife, as well as when Gabe positioned himself alongside with waiting boot. Then there was nothing in the world but that muzzle and Sorrels's doomed eyes. They were the same as Tom knew his own to be, windows into a dark soul that already had so much to answer for. But after what had happened at Horsehead Crossing, Tom figured one more killing wouldn't much affect his chances for forgiveness anyway.

With a deep breath, he tightened his finger against the trigger.

A splatter like water against rock breached the fortress of Tom's concentration. He whirled, finding Jess's blade rising against the throat of a horse whose urine streamed downward.

"Hold that knife!" Tom rasped. "Get your boot under him!"

Jess and Gabe swung around simultaneously, then Gabe was diving under the appaloosa and searching for its discolored stream.

"Got it!" cried Gabe, catching as much on his arm as he did the boot. "Pee away, Pretty Butt ol' boy!"

"Gotta do the same for these others!" Jess shouted, reeling toward another gelding. He tried to yank his boot off a little too soon and fell at the hoofs of the paint. "Sorrels! Get to a horse!"

Tom turned back to Sorrels's stunned and confused features and made him look into the .44's bore for anxious moments longer.

"Young fellow gets first drink," Tom warned, "or I swear to God I'll still do it!"

Tom withdrew, and Gabe collected the appaloosa's flow and hurried to Dee. Tom would have met him there to help, but he had already taken up a position under another animal. Through its forelegs, he watched Gabe lift the boy's head and tilt the boot to his lips.

"Little at a time!" Tom cautioned in the mere whisper he could manage.

Tom wanted to see if the kid responded, but he felt sudden moisture against his fingers and began to catch the bay's stream. Tom had never seen urine so black, or smelled any so putrid, but it was wet and running and filling his cracked boot on up to the upper that flopped to the side. He hadn't anticipated much of a yield and lost some in his haste to pull off his other boot, but he nevertheless captured a near boot-full and part of another.

As he scooted into the open, spilling a little in his weakness-induced awkwardness, Tom realized there was a reason why man or animal urinated. It was a way of flushing poisons, and he didn't know if drinking it would stave off death or just hasten it. Either way, he figured, it had to be better than a lingering end under the sun.

Looking about, he saw Gabe rise from a stirring Dee and lift a sloshing boot to his mouth. But it wasn't until Gabe delivered the boot to Jess that Tom closed his eyes and raised the disgusting brew to his lips. He braced himself, trying not to think about its origin, then the hot liquid was pouring down his parched throat, an incredibly bitter and salty potion that kicked him in the gut.

He thought he would vomit, but somehow the urine stayed down even as his stomach seemed to turn inside out. He drank more and more, before passing the fuller boot to Gabe to share with Dee and Jess. Tom kept the other and started to partake again, but just as he brought the leather to his mouth he saw Sorrels drop to both knees before him.

Tom had never seen lips so cracked or trembling. He had never known a face at once so burned and pale, or eyes so bloodshot and pitiful. Sorrels's were the features of a dying man reduced to beggar, and without another sip Tom extended the boot.

He could always kill him later, if he had to. Right now, though, that extra gun Sorrels offered had reassumed an importance that might eventually prove just as critical as drink.

The four of them monitored the horses without reward for another half-hour before the necessity of making miles in the cooler hours drove them to the trail. Tom had never felt so sick to his stomach, and he figured his breath reeked as much as his boots, sticky against his feet. For fifteen minutes after drinking, the urine had quenched his thirst, but now the brine lingered in his throat and made him yearn for water even more. Still, he was sweating again, just as the silvery beads had also returned to Dee's face.

The boy wasn't exactly conscious, but at least Tom had less trouble supporting him now as they doubled-up on the big bay. Tom, too, whether from sun or dehydration or horse urine, was far from clear-headed, for he had plenty of reason to expect the worst if he failed to reckon with Sorrels's Winchester.

Tom's first inkling that he was in trouble came with Jess's quick "Watch out!"

Tom looked around simultaneous with the boom of a rifle and saw Jess wheeling his roan and struggling to pull his revolver out of his waistband. Then pain told Tom that something

140

had branded him in the shoulder, for it burned like singed cowhide. At the same time his arm went weak, almost causing him to yield his grip on Dee. Then Jess had that .41 out and leveled on something behind Tom.

"Put it down!" cried Jess.

Tom pivoted his bay to smell gun smoke and stare into the dark muzzle of Sorrels's shouldered Winchester a horse-length away. Unintentionally, Tom had positioned Dee as a shield between himself and that rifle.

"You better not miss," said Tom. "Hurt him any and by God I'll do worse'n any Comanche butchers ever thought of doin'."

"For God's sake, put it down!" Jess told Sorrels again.

Still, Sorrels's squinted eyes stayed behind the Winchester's barrel. "Son bitch already tried killin' me twice! Ain't givin' him a third chance!"

"Yeah? You killin' me too?" demanded Jess. "That's what it's gonna take!"

"I'm doin' what I have to!"

From off to the side, Gabe's shotgun began to rise. "Not a good idea, Sorrels," said Gabe, cocking both hammers. "Even for somebody with the brains of a cow pile."

Sorrels glanced from Gabe to Jess and back to Tom in tense cycle, his eyes like the flashing of shuffled cards. Tom knew that the longer the standoff persisted, the greater the chance for the twitch of a trigger finger, with far-reaching consequences. Not only would it send him to Sarah sooner that he had expected, it would also set off a chain of events that would all but seal that seventeen-year-old girl's fate.

With an oath, Sorrels lowered the Winchester. "The whole lot of you's ganged up on me!"

"We got Liz Anne to think about," said Jess, keeping his six-shooter on him. "Don't go thinkin' I won't do what I got to either. Gabe, get that rifle of his."

Gabe urged his horse over and reached for the Winchester. "Come here, ol' 'Chester. Meet my little scatter gun."

Grudgingly, Sorrels yielded the weapon. "You're a bunch of damned fools! Catch them Meskins and you're gonna need all the firepower you can muster!"

"Better think about that yourself next time you're fixin' to back-shoot somebody," said Jess. He took his horse around the nose of Tom's bay. "Tom, let's see that arm."

Only now did Tom inspect his shoulder to find a dark, moist rip in his shirt. The cloth was half-glued to the skin by blood, but Jess peeled it away to reveal a shallow cut without entry or exit wound.

"Needs cleanin'," said Jess, "but that'll have to wait on water."

"Obliged you hollerin' when you did," Tom said, adding another name to his indebtedness. "Some strips left in my war bag, if you can dig 'em out for me. Don't want to lose my hold on the young fellow here."

Jess complied, but his attention seemed divided as he glanced over his shoulder at Sorrels.

"Tom, what you want to do about this?" he asked in a subdued voice.

"Just bandage me up best you can."

"I mean Sorrels. He just tried—"

"See that ridge way yonder? We don't make it over them mountains, what he done ain't gonna make a bit of difference. Just fix me up and we'll give it our best, all the way to the end."

TWELVE

The gray escarpment across the horizon never seemed to get nearer as the morning sun tortured Jess's back like a bellows-fanned blacksmith fire. As dehydrated as he was, he still held out hope that the horse urine of sunup would see the five of them through those mountains and on to the river. But so much depended on their mounts, which had now been pushed hard without water or forage for more than forty-eight hours. Broken down by chase and distance, storm and sun, they were mere scarecrows, bereft of both flesh and spirit.

Still, hoof after slow hoof reached out relentlessly along a rock-scored trail.

If there was just a shade somewhere, a place to hole up and unsaddle the animals and rest them till nightfall . . . Only then would Jess have bet even a wooden nickel on the likelihood of anyone surviving.

Liz Anne.

He shuddered in sudden memory of the glimpse he'd had of her through the dust. Her only chance rested in the five of them and their horses—and that chance was dying more and more surely with every passing second under a heartless sun.

Gabe's paint began to lag, and Jess dropped back and inspected the struggling mount.

"Pony's got the creeps," said Jess as he came abreast.

"Hell, Jess, they's plum' rode down, ever' last one," Gabe rasped impatiently. "Damned crow-baits, they are. Hellfire, ain't you got eyes?"

It was the first time Jess had ever heard him curse, but Gabe wasn't finished.

"We let them SOBs sucker us into followin' out here, and we've played the fool right up to a three-by-six hole in the ground."

"They got Liz Anne, Gabe," Jess reminded.

Gabe pulled rein, leading Jess to do the same, and the two men faced one another.

"They got her, all right, Jess, and that ain't ever gonna change. We'll all be dead as old man Buckalew and she'll be worse than dead. It was set in stone the moment they rode off with her. You was a fool chasin' after her, but I was a bigger one for ever' comin' with you."

A little stunned, Jess could only stare into a pair of sunken eyes maybe only a few blinks from death. He and Gabe had worked side-by-side for three different outfits and had never had a cross word.

"I . . . I'm sorry you feel that a-way, Gabe," he finally managed. "You and me's rode the river a bunch of years."

"I ain't some yearlin' you slapped your brand on just so's I could follow you around."

"I know you ain't, Gabe. Maybe . . . Maybe I been dead wrong thinkin' we could get her back. Maybe we're all fixin' to die out here, just like you say."

"Sure as that sun's a-shinin'."

"But if we are, Gabe, don't forget I made it plain to you and ever'body else back at headquarters. Your job as a 7L hand stopped right there, and from there on out it was up to what you decided as a man."

Jess didn't even wait to see Gabe's reaction. He eased his horse ahead, but now he carried an extra burden that seemed to rob him of the little hope from which he had drawn strength.

As the shadows of yucca shrank close to the stems, the bayonet leaves began to dance around Jess like twirling knives. He couldn't stop the dizzying whirl of land and sky and sun, and the only way to stay on his horse was to close his eyes and hump up over the saddle horn.

He didn't want to die with regrets, but plenty of them rode with him. From out of his past, he lamented again holding his silence when he had peered through that cracked shed wall. From the here and now, he bemoaned that he and Gabe couldn't at least die as compadres after living as such all these years. But what he regretted most was failing Liz Anne and denying her the future she deserved, no matter if he was a part of it or not.

He sank deeper and deeper into a stupor from which he knew he would never return. His bones would mark this trail the same as so many others, and no one who passed would ever hear their silent cry of anguish for an innocent girl whose chances had died with him.

Suddenly Jess seemed to topple into a great spinning funnel, and even after something rushed up and struck him a stunning blow, this wildest ride of his life just kept going on and on. In his fog, he imagined dampness against his cheek, and he opened his eyes to a dark blur and the smell of fresh dirt.

Jess's vertigo was as severe as ever, but he summoned enough awareness to realize that he had tumbled from his horse. But what was he to make of the way the soil wrapped around his jaw and hugged his shoulder? Or of the nearby cry of exaltation?

He tasted moistness on his lips, and he turned his head just enough to feel something smooth and wet against his tongue. It seemed to act as a stimulant, and he came to an elbow to find himself in a mud hole sheltered from the sky. His horse was above him, pawing at the ground, and past a dangling stirrup he could see the meeting of two rock walls, a looming fort in stark contrast to the angling shadows below it. Tasajillo pushed against its base, while from a jagged crack halfway to the top a stunted prickly pear clung precariously.

That was all Jess could do as well, cling precariously to fragile life. But to another cry from Sorrels, he got his knees under him and began to crawl for the wettest spot he saw, a low place with a sheen as glossy as the Concho bend where he and Liz Anne had camped. Sorrels was already sprawled there, scooping mud into his mouth and choking on it.

The forelegs of a bay passed at Jess's flank, followed by more hoofs that bogged, and he glanced over to see Gabe reaching to assist Dee from Tom's horse. Then Jess was alongside Sorrels and digging in sticky alkali that oozed between his fingers.

From Sorrels he had learned not to feed on the mud, but as he scratched deeper and deeper, the seepage he hoped to generate just wouldn't come. Teased and denied at death's brink, he looked up in despair to see Tom collapse at his shoulder.

Jess no longer had the strength for coherent words, so he watched in silent pity as the confused old man struggled with button after button and removed his linsey-woolsey shirt.

Funny how a dying man's mind worked, thought Jess, for Tom proceeded to unfurl the garment along the ground and pile it with the wettest mud he could find. It was so tragically child-like, yet Tom worked diligently, finally drawing the corners together and sealing them with a twist. Lifting the mass overhead, Tom wrung it with both hands, straining a trickle of precious water that he caught between burned lips.

Pity, hell! thought Jess. This was one old cow-hand who refused to go silently into the night. The next instant, Jess was fumbling with his own buttons, but he had so little dexterity left that Tom was already at work on a second shirt-full by the time Jess folded his first.

The 7L boss initially managed only a few drops across his tongue, but he found greater reward when he pressed the wadded material to his lips. Squeezing and sucking, he could taste the salt of his sweat-stained shirt, but it came with sip after sip of water. When the first batch of mud could yield no more, he started in on a second portion, then a third and a fourth. He didn't think he would ever slake his thirst, but as soon as he collected mud for the fifth time, he turned with his wadded shirt and started on hands and knees for Dee.

Tom was already there, hovering over the supine boy and wrenching out a discolored trickle that found Dee's responsive lips. Still, Jess continued his painful crawl, knowing that Dee would need much, much more.

Perez rode numb to everything but the gash in his cheek. It cut so deeply that he could poke his tongue through from inside out and taste the blood. There was no other way he had of moistening his mouth, although doing so stirred pain as searing as the overhead sun.

Perez had the hellcat to thank for his misery. He almost wished that her revolver shot had caught him flush rather than merely grazed, for then he wouldn't have to face this terrifying sea—a sea of bare alkali with bone-like rocks shining in the late morning.

He had never lamented the loss of two of his men, except as gun hands, for the old gringo who had raised him had taught him well what it was to be uncaring. But selfish regret had begun to consume Perez. He could have held to petty thievery in Coahuila and contented himself in tequila and whores, rather than ride a trail through purgatory with a white girl in tow and two cabrons abreast.

Between the sun and his unknown pursuers, he just didn't know if he could get out of this alive. It was the hellcat's fault, all of it, and if he didn't survive, he would see to it in his last breath that she didn't either. That moment might be fast approaching, for Perez had to find drink—and there were no more spare horses to bleed out.

He had stayed in the stirrups all through a night so dark at times that only the squeak of other saddles and tramping of adjacent hoofs had assured him he wasn't alone. Then the sun had burned away the gloom, but a greater one had taken its place to steal away little by little the last of his hope.

Across Perez's path darted a sudden, winged shadow, a black visitor staining the glare on the desert floor. The shadow cut the alkali a second time, then a third, and he looked up over his shoulder to see a buzzard wheeling through the sky.

With an oath, Perez yanked out his revolver. Already, it seemed, death had begun, and it promised to end with claws in his flesh and a rapier-like beak pecking out his eyes.

"*Fuera de aqui!*" he cried, firing a wild shot into the sun just as wings eclipsed it.

But rather than go away, the vulture burst out of

the fiery swell, a harbinger of death circling and waiting.

With continued cries Perez fired again, and the buzzard swerved. He discharged the remaining rounds in quick succession and saw a puff of feathers dust the sky, sending those effortlessly gliding wings into an erratic downward spiral. The vulture was still flapping its good appendage when it crashed through a nearby stand of prickly pear that came alive, a stirring mass of feathers and cactus pads subject to talons and spines.

With a half-laugh of surprise, Perez exchanged glances with Rodriguez and Ernesto, but then he laughed no more.

In those hardened, desperate eyes he saw the same thought that abruptly seized his every fiber. The carrion eater trapped in that cactus meant blood—foul blood, all right, but maybe enough to sustain life for one person and one alone.

He swung his leg over the cantle and stepped off in such a frenzy that he failed to reckon with a stirrup holding fast a left foot that he didn't have the strength to remove. He fell hard, losing reins and tow rope both, but at least his boot slipped free. Struggling up, he staggered after the two Mexicans who rushed ahead for the scavenger.

"*Alto! Alto!*" he shouted.

But Rodriguez and Ernesto were too busy jostling shoulders and throwing elbows in a stumbling race. Again Perez yelled for the two to stop, but their instinct for survival took precedence over the force of his will.

Perez still had his revolver in hand, and he lifted the muzzle against those weaving backs before realizing he had already emptied the cylinder. Now his profanity reached new heights, for he could only thrust the barrel back in his waistband and watch helplessly as the men waded one after the other into cactus that met them chest high.

The dust devil of spines and talons repelled Rodriguez first, and then a cursing Ernesto. Moaning and checking their wounds, they seemed oblivious to Perez as he charged. He broke between the two, knocking one to the left and the other to the right, and lunged for the only hope he had left.

He fell upon cactus and buzzard, a hundred needles piercing him. Blunt talons strafed his face as a hissing demon with a horrible stench and a six-foot wingspan engaged him as if guarding hell's gate. He fended off a powerful wing flailing at his skull and came eye to eye with gray-brown irises peering evilly out of a blood-red crown. A hooked beak as pale as death snapped forward, and Perez's vision blurred. Suddenly droplets were flying, more and more with every flash of a beak turning dark and moist.

The vulture was literally eating him alive, the most horrible end Perez could imagine, but somehow he closed his hand around the pliable neck. He managed to unsheathe his knife and slash away at feather and bone, but talons and wings continued to punish him until he hacked off the head.

Perez lost his grip and the decapitated fowl dropped, thrashing wildly and slinging precious blood. Seizing it by the breast and a wing, he closed his teeth over the gushing neck and lifted the stained plumage overhead. A five-pound vulture had little blood to give, and the very thought of drinking it was revolting, but Perez reveled in every warm, syrupy drop that coated his throat. When the flow was exhausted, he disemboweled the scavenger and found additional fluids, although they proved so putrid that he tossed the remains to Rodriguez and Ernesto.

Until now, desperation and the rush of battle had muted Perez's pain, but agony overwhelmed him as he picked his way into the open. He wanted to collapse and writhe in the dirt, but to do so would only drive the spines deeper. His only option was to double over groaning, although when he did so the close-up view of all the needles protruding from sleeve and pants leg only heightened his anguish. Almost mercifully, a mist clouded Perez's vision, and he brushed his brow to find blood on his hand. Maybe the buzzard had given him a few additional hours of life, but he wondered if it hadn't robbed him of even more.

Perez set about pulling the larger spines from

his forearms and thighs, and just when he thought he was making progress he found a pin cushion of needles in his buttocks. He knew he could ill afford to ride in such a condition, for as soon as he climbed into the saddle—

Caballo!

Perez had been so obsessed with reaching the buzzard ahead of Rodriguez and Ernesto that he hadn't taken time to secure his animal. If it had wandered away, the consequences could be dire.

Perez whirled, intent on seizing another's mount if necessary. Yards away, his all-but-dead animal still stood in place, bait for the next circling buzzard. But *Ay Dios*! The hellcat was gone!

Perez squinted as he scanned the flats. He thought he glimpsed something off to the south, but it disappeared in an abrupt fog in his eyes. He rubbed his bleeding brow into his shoulder and winced to the painful drag of a spine across his eyelids. By the time he stifled the flow enough to see, there were only yucca and tasajillo all the way to the horizon. But as he continued to pivot in the dirt, he caught a wisp of dust against the purplish ridge that, ever since sunup, had grown in prominence in the west with every stride of his horse.

The hellcat!

It took all of Perez's energy just to put one foot after the other, but he managed to reach his horse. Mounting up offered an even greater challenge, for no matter how many times he rocked with a boot in the stirrup and a hand on the horn, he couldn't muster the strength to step up. Finally he led the black to a fallen yucca that elevated him just enough to gain the saddle.

Perez wheeled the horse and gigged it after the girl, but she had a quarter-mile lead and his animal had little to give. He slipped his quirt off the horn and whipped the black again and again, but no degree of abuse could transform a broken-down pony into a racehorse. At least he managed to coax the gelding into a fast walk, although the bouncing gait so aggravated Perez's wounded buttocks that he was forced to half-stand in the stirrups and pick spines as he rode. The position tortured his quivering knees, but he was finally able to bear full weight and concentrate on that receding puff of dust.

Twice now the girl had tried to escape, and Perez knew that to give chase this time was to risk killing his horse and dying alongside it. Still, he pushed on, driven by all that had gone on before.

Perez's entire life had been fragmented, a broken series of incidents involving an alcoholic whore of a mother, a domineering old gringo, and sordid criminality that had kept him a mere step ahead of a federales firing squad. He had never had the kind of stability and nurturing that engendered perseverance, but an unquenchable yearning for acceptance had taught him grim determination in all things related to greed. The girl represented money, a lot of it, and Perez was not unaware that the most highly respected men in Mexico were of wealth. He didn't know the price of respect in terms of pesos, but delivering the girl to a rich patron would at least set him on his way.

Before long, Perez's horse stumbled and couldn't regain its previous stride, despite another fierce quirting. He trailed by several hundred yards now, but he saw the girl glance back and ease her mount into a slow walk that would keep her well out of pistol range. Forced to settle into a battle of wills and horses, Perez at least took heart in knowing that the girl held to the old road that was said to lead to the waters of Rio Pecos.

THIRTEEN

The shallow water hole, a sloughed earthen cistern evidently muddied by the previous day's storm, promised Tom and his companions more than it could deliver, especially with so many competing hands and hoofs. All too soon, they had no choice but to seek out the shady ruins.

Twenty years ago, Tom had figured this structure for another old mail station, a fort twenty paces long and ten paces wide with stacked limestone walls almost twice a man's height. The outpost had been largely intact back then, but through an open gateway now sprawled a cacti-infested courtyard fronted by crumbling rooms open to the sky. The effects of wind, rain, and time had breached the courtyard walls, most notably where a deep V framed the Castle Mountains ridge that finally had grown to significant size. Still, sufficient rock remained to hold jaded mounts and cast shadows, although it was no easy task for men who could barely walk to unsaddle and turn the horses inside.

As the tender-footed animals retreated from a midday sun hotter than ever, Tom helped string a catch-rope across the entrance and sank beside Jess under a dark perimeter wall. Tom reckoned that the hewn blocks of limestone were at least twenty degrees cooler here on the fort's north side, where sunlight seldom struck, but the dehydrating air seemed to boil as intensely as ever.

Dee, stretched out on the other side of Jess, moaned in delirium, but at least he exhibited more life than he had since the black of early morning. Beyond slumped Gabe, his forearms across uplifted knees as he hung his head in the same muteness that had characterized him ever since Tom had overheard him exchange words with Jess. Farther away, Sorrels brooded apart from the group, but not so far as to be forgotten again.

Realizing their only chance was to travel by

night, Tom welcomed the shade, but he hated the wall that cast it. The stacked blocks loomed over him like a great tombstone, now as it had then. If only he and the other teamsters had recognized it as a cairn on the road to hell. If only they had turned back and fled into the dusk. If only . . . if only . . .

Instead they had embraced these walls and made camp, fools persisting in fools' folly. In this very spot he and Sarah had stretched their bedding, finding false security in a bulwark of cut lime-stone. Even when the eighteen-month-old girl had taken ill in the night and died before daybreak, no one had accepted it as the dark omen it was. Out behind these leering walls, Tom had helped bury her at first light—a happy little girl with all the promise of a future one moment, and a cold, stiff bundle robbed of everything the next.

"Awful sad place, this is."

Tom didn't realize he had spoken aloud until he noticed Jess studying him.

"They's a grave out back," Tom added.

"A grave?"

"I didn't see it neither, but it's there. Scratched her name on a rock myself."

"Whose name?"

Tom coughed, trying to clear the alkali, but only a hoarse whisper would crawl up from his larynx. "Year and a half old. Mama and daddy wasn't hardly growed themselves. Helluva place to leave your little girl."

Tom picked up the course of a whirlwind a couple of hundred yards away and remembered as he watched.

"How come her to die?" asked Jess.

The pint-sized cyclone advanced, a twisting funnel dancing among the yucca.

"Taken the cholera."

Jess shook his head. "Didn't have a chance then."

"Liked to got caught under a wheel second day out of San Antone. Shoulda took it as a sign and turned back. There on out, the company women took turns a-carryin' her."

"What call you have to be with a wagon train, Tom?"

At first Tom hesitated, the bad memories too strong, but the walls had sparked such a powerful connection with the past that the images began to flow into words.

"Seventeen of us, they was. Indians had took these parts over after the war. Damned fools we was, thinkin' we could fight 'em off. Told her, once we get to the Pecos, they'd leave us be."

"Told who?"

Abruptly the whirlwind seemed to spirit away all of Tom's long-ago dreams. "Month or two along already when we started out. She walked with the sickness ever mornin'. Time we got to

159

Horsehead, camped around a oxbow bend from them 'dobe walls, she was awful weakly. Turned our stock out to graze and sat around talkin' names, the two of us. We both figured it for a boy."

"She's the girl you talked about, then. The one you loved."

The whirlwind against the sky seemed to change shape, the swirls coalescing into something dark and evil as Tom re-lived that day on the treeless Pecos banks.

"They come outa nowhere, hoofs a-thunderin'. Must've been a hundred of them Comanches. You could see 'em scowlin' behind the war paint, their feathers a-wavin'. They opened up on us, and we went to shootin' back. But they wasn't but six of us had arms, and two of them was with the herd.

" 'Fore we turned them Indians, they'd cut down three of us. All we could do was leave 'em and run a wagon across a washout for a fort. The dust and smoke wouldn't settle 'fore they'd come at us again, the bullets a-whizzin'. Time they backed off and run them cattle across the ford, we was just three able-bodied men and two women.

"We loaded them others that wasn't dead and made for them mud walls, draggin' that wagon by the tongue. Them Indians done took ever'thing we had, but that wasn't enough for 'em. They caught us in the open right there at that oxbow, and all we could do was leave the wounded to die and try to fight our way on across. All I was hopin' was they'd kill her first, so I could die knowin' they couldn't do worse to her.

"Took a bullet in my knee, but there she was, helpin' me over them fallin' walls, that old stage stand. I went to layin' down fire so's more of us could make it, but the last two dropped face-down not twenty steps away. I went to reloadin' and them Comanches scalped 'em right in front of our eyes."

Tom turned away and fell silent, but the memories continued to scream.

"My Lord, Tom, my Lord," muttered Jess. "The hands on herd, whatever—"

"Mighty awful what we seen. Tied them poor men to wagon wheels just out of range. Went to cuttin' on 'em, men we knowed just a-cryin' the most pitiful cries you ever heard. Soon's good dark hit, they was still alive, but them devils drenched 'em with kerosene and they just went to blazin'."

"Shut him up!" Sorrels blurted. "Shut that old man up!"

Tom looked over, past a pale Jess and an even more ashen Gabe. Sorrels's eyes were wide and wild and gripped by deep-rooted fear.

"Ain't it enough we're dyin'?" Sorrels went on. "We gotta listen to him make it worse?"

"Might pay to listen to him," spoke up Jess. "Knows how to get out of a fix alive, or he wouldn't be here."

"Yeah? Maybe he went to killin' his own bunch like he nearly done me. Maybe he forced that woman to run for it so's he could swim the river. Maybe the coward got her shot dead, same as if he'd pulled the trigger hisself."

The whirlwind was upon Tom, attacking with swirling grit that stung and blinded, but a far greater fury boiled up inside him. While instinct cried out that he turn away, a rage more consuming than any he had ever known brought him jerking his Colt out of its holster.

He cocked it even as he leveled the barrel across the line of Jess's outstretched legs. The 7L boss was distinct enough, shielding his face from the storm, but everything beyond was no better defined than ribbons of smoke. But Tom knew where the wall stood, and where it ended, and he made a quick guess at Sorrels's exact location and squeezed the trigger.

The blast seemed to sweep the dust devil away, leaving Tom looking down the barrel at a startled Sorrels.

"What in hell—"

Tom didn't know if the cry came from Sorrels or Jess, or both of them together, but it was Sorrels who recoiled and began scrambling away on all fours. There was no evidence that a bullet had winged him, but Tom didn't intend to miss with the next one.

He spun another live round into the chamber as

he struggled to his feet, but his legs were so weak that he was off-balance as he fired again. By then, Sorrels was scurrying around the corner, but shrapnel flew in his wake as a bullet exploded against the fort's edge and ricocheted.

"Damn it, Tom! What are you—"

Tom paid Jess no attention as he stumbled down the row of cowhands and cocked his six-shooter a third time. He'd kill the bastard! He'd gut-shoot the son of a bitch or put a bullet between his eyes or square in his back, but he swore he'd kill him!

"Tom! Tom!"

He heard Jess's cry as if from afar, but there was nothing distant about the sudden hand on his shoulder. Tom whirled, his anger unchecked, and the barrel of his .44 whirled with him. Jess was there, palms outward in supplication.

"It's me, Tom! Tom, it's me!"

Tom saw the concern in the stubbly face, the plea in the bloodshot eyes.

"Don't get in my way, son," Tom rasped. "Just don't get in my way."

"I got to, Tom. I got to, 'cause I don't know what's happened all of a sudden."

"Only way you're gonna stop me is to kill me. You do what you got to, 'cause that's what I'm a-doin'."

Tom turned and staggered on to the shattered block with its fresh, white sheen. He burst around the corner and the sun's fiery rays struck him a punishing blow. Still, he kept on, steadying himself with a hand against searing rock. He saw no sign of Sorrels, but he could hear Jess continue to call as if across a gulf of twenty years.

"I need you, Tom! I need you both to get Liz Anne back!"

But the blood fever ran too hot through Tom's veins, blinding him to everything except shutting Sorrels up once and for all. He turned the far corner and saw Sorrels retreating into the scattered yucca. The 7L hand was a few yards out of pistol range, but Tom nevertheless took aim as Sorrels looked back over his shoulder.

The instant the percussion cap exploded, Sorrels stumbled over a hewn block burning white in the sun. The pistol ball must have clipped the isolated rock and changed course, for the adjacent succulents began to sing as Sorrels went down.

He had him! The red devil had tripped on his face and he had him!

To guarantee it, though, Tom had to stay upright long enough to struggle a few steps farther with his battle-worn six-shooter. The bulge in the barrel could send a shot wide, but a ball fired at close range would be just as deadly as the one that had taken Sarah.

The moment Tom drew back the hammer, a quick constriction struck his chest. Reflexively, he fired off a wild shot. Then the growing tightness doubled him over, the revolver falling from his hand.

Virtually immobilized, he sank to his knees. Still, he willed himself to reach for the .44, glinting on the ground so near and yet so far. But the pain seemed bent on wrenching from him what little life he had left, and he was powerless to do anything but sag to his shoulder and lie there gripping his chest.

"My Lord, Tom, what—"

Jess was suddenly kneeling before him, blocking the sun and placing a gentle hand on his shoulder. Tom began to wallow in the dirt, but he had learned from experience to endure in silence. The spells were seizing him with greater frequency, more intensity, but he knew that if he could just weather this one long enough, it too might pass like the others.

And he could still join Sarah at those executioner's walls on the Pecos.

"Can you get a breath?" pressed Jess. "Talk to me—you able to talk to me?"

With Jess's every movement, the sun either blinded or disappeared, and Tom lifted a hand more as a shield than as a reply.

"Tom, I'm gonna get you back in the shade." Jess's silhouette turned away for a moment. "Gabe! Gabe! Get over here!"

Resting his head on the scorching ground, Tom closed his eyes and tolled off the brutal seconds that came and went without relief. Maybe the catch-rope around his torso would never go slack. Maybe a dead man's hand had been dealt him before he could atone for his sin at Horsehead Crossing. Maybe fate had been cruel enough to lure him all this way, only to deny him those final moments in communion with Sarah.

When he opened his eyes, his field of vision was limited to a few feet of alkali and that glaring crease of sun on the cylinder of his revolver. Then scuffed boots were there as well, and a hand that darted down for the weapon's dusty grip.

"Leave it!"

Jess's frantic cry precipitated a blur of pivoting boots and lunging arms. Suddenly two very different hands closed on the revolver, but only one index finger penetrated the trigger guard. The muzzle began to sweep one way and then another as a pair of dark shapes wrestled against the sun.

"Give it up!" cried Jess. "Give it up!"

Tom saw the hammer spring back a little, then yawn again. With the kind of pressure the index finger exerted on the trigger, he knew it was only a matter of time before—

The ground exploded before Tom, strafing his leg with dirt as thunder reverberated. For a moment the discharge seemed to stun everyone, for two sets of hands froze on the Colt. Then a vicious leg whip took one man's feet out from under him, and a single hand broke free with the revolver.

The muzzle surged straight for Tom.

"Don't look like so much now, do you?" growled Sorrels, cocking the weapon. "See you in h—"

Boom!

The startling blast of a shotgun cut Sorrels short and kept his finger from squeezing the trigger. Tom looked around with him to see Gabe emerging from around the corner as the twin barrels of his twelve-gauge quickly went from skyward to horizontal.

"Ol' scatter gun's still got one barrel to go," Gabe told Sorrels. "I'm figurin' you oughta drop that thing."

"He's lookin' to kill me!" contended Sorrels.

Gabe continued to approach, keeping the barrels trained on the man behind the revolver.

"Sorrels, I'm out here where I wish I ain't, the coffin maker's done measured me for a fit, and I got a saddle sore where the sun don't shine. I expect you better listen to me, 'cause I'm sure 'nough ready to take it out on somebody."

Sorrels lowered the Colt, then Jess was on his feet before him.

"Old man's crazy!" said Sorrels as Jess snatched the weapon from his hand. "He's crazy as you are for chasin' after that little wh—"

The .44 barrel swung upward until the muzzle was in Sorrels's paling face.

"You disrespectful bastard!" cried Jess, his gun hand shaking with rage. "This thing's still cocked!"

Sorrels lowered his gaze and slunk away. Tom expected no less; he was a back-shooting coward.

Just as Gabe came up, the band across Tom's chest began to ease and he realized his list of debtors was growing.

"Obliged," he managed.

"Lots of folks oughta be," said Gabe with a glance toward Jess. "Still don't mean we's gettin' out of this alive."

FOURTEEN

They were dead men riding dead horses through the gloom of night.

At dusk Jess had dragged himself into the saddle and turned his mount after the others down a last-chance trail. Now he rocked to the roan's creeping gait, but when he closed his eyes he seemed to float rather than ride. All his senses seemed a half-step off stride, as if he were an observer of this scene instead of an actor, but he was lucid enough to consider this entire ordeal's effect on everyone.

With those murderers ahead, Jess knew that he would need every gun hand he could muster. But how could he hope to hold this bunch together?

Tom wanted to kill Sorrels, Sorrels wanted to kill Tom, and Gabe didn't want to have anything to do with any of them. Meanwhile, poor Dee was suffering terribly, moaning as he rode in Tom's arms. Hell, all of them were suffering, and if something didn't change soon, Gabe would damned sure be proven right about their fate.

Jess had a lot of concerns, but he dwelled mostly on Tom, whose face, in Jess's stupor, strangely seemed to take on characteristics of his father's. When the old cowhand had whispered of the little girl and all the events that had followed, Jess had caught himself wondering how much of it was a big windy. But right before sunset, he had wandered out back to the hewn block scarred by Tom's pistol ball. The rock stood at the head of a small, sunken grave from which a mesquite seedling had sprouted. The name was indecipherable, but when he read the age—eighteen months —he had no more reason for doubt.

Whatever Tom's demons, they had been forged at least in part by this trail.

Still, Jess couldn't understand Tom's motivation for suddenly firing at Sorrels, but it didn't take much in the way of smarts for the wagon boss to realize he had better keep Tom's .44 and Dee's .45 in his waistband for now. Tom, in his sickness and exhaustion, hadn't asked for his weapon back yet, but Jess knew it was only a matter of time. He dreaded the moment, for if he were to alienate his greatest ally, he might have to stand up against a horde of butchers all on his own.

But with the old cowhand liable to keel over at any second, just how much difference would it make anyway?

From abreast, Jess could hear Tom's and Dee's spurs jingling to their horse's slow gait. He opened his eyes to find the two in the muted light of a nearly full moon rising at their backs.

"Dee doin' good as he can?"

Tom's daze must have been as great as Jess's, for the spurs rattled on for several seconds before he answered.

"Asked for his mama a ways back."

"Poor little dogie," sympathized Jess. "So out of it, don't even know she's been gone for years."

"They don't never leave us, son. If you ever once loved somebody, they's always there with us."

Jess hung his head. His father was still with him, all right, crying out for help with a .44 muzzle at his temple.

Tom began to cough weakly, drawing Jess's attention. The rising dust was bad enough on Jess, but Tom continued to hack as if it threatened to shut off his air.

"You all right?"

Tom's cough persisted for a few strides more. "Nothin' a big swallow couldn't fix."

Jess had a good idea that not even water could address all of Tom's ailments.

"How long you been havin' these spells, Tom?"

"Alkali's bad about that."

"I mean back at the walls. You know."

Tom didn't answer, but Jess pressed the issue. "Tom?"

"Long enough."

"Seen a doctor?"

Tom coughed again. "Don't need one. All I need's to get to Horsehead Crossin' after we get that girl back."

Jess was almost afraid to follow up, fearing that he might inadvertently set Tom off again. But he asked anyway.

"How come you goin' back there?"

"Told you already."

"You mean about seein' the girl you loved once?"

Again the only reply was the jingle of spurs and clomp of hoofs.

"Tom? She . . . She's dead, ain't she."

Still Tom rode in silence.

"Payin' your respects at her grave, I reckon," Jess suggested.

"Somethin' like that."

Remembering how he had twice found Tom with his forehead resting against the barrel of a .44, Jess wondered just how much this haunted man might have in common with his father.

Already, Liz Anne regretted her decision.

Maybe if her shot had done more than graze

171

Perez, she would have felt differently. Maybe if she had succeeded in ridding the world of this lowest form of vermin, it would have been worth living this hell that would always be her life. But she had merely wounded, and however sinister Perez had been before, the torture to which her bullet subjected him had summoned up an evil twice as bad.

She rode with a quarter-mile lead that never seemed to change, but it was a fragile advantage that could disappear in a hurry. Any moment, her faltering horse could go down and she would be at his mercy again. She wouldn't even be able to flee on foot, for her hands were still tied to the saddle horn.

For hours now, ever since the Mexicans had forgotten her in the vulture's shadow, she had gnawed at the rope. Her teeth ached, and her bleeding gums had smeared the fibers red, but still the knot held. Jess had told her once how a coyote would gnaw off its foot to escape a steel trap, but what would freedom gain her when Perez had already taken her very future?

Jess.

He would never know how close she held him in her heart in these awful times. His face dominated her thoughts, stirring both hope and despair. As much as she wanted him to ride Perez down and take vengeance for her father's last moments, she wanted more that Jess never know what had happened to her in the hellfire glow of the burning house.

Now another blaze from perdition had just sunk behind the nearing mountains, leaving in its wake a sky painted fiery orange. Her Virginia-raised father had often said that West Texas had the most beautiful sunsets, but this one seemed to usher in a gloom even more frightful than the one that had gripped her for three days now.

She had no place to go, no reason for being, but the skeleton between her legs kept carrying her along in its painful march. The horse traced the old wagon ruts down into a shallow valley dotted with dirt mounds as far as she could see. Her addled senses took the scene for a cemetery, and as the too-small graves crept up on all sides, they seemed to reach out for her like hants. They were there, all right, wraiths seeking to drag her down to a grave not of her choosing.

"Get away!"

Liz Anne gigged the horse and the animal bolted with a hidden reserve that surprised her. The bay achieved only a trot, but it was through a perilous bottom riddled not just with mounds but hoof-sized holes.

In a dark corner of her mind, she recognized this as an old prairie dog town, a place through which even the most forked rider knew to pick his way carefully. Not only could an errant hoof find a burrow, but prairie dogs were notorious for digging upward-trending escape tunnels that ended only inches from the surface—sure-fire traps for any horse and rider.

The trouble was, confusion and flesh-crawling fear overwhelmed that dark recess in Liz Anne's mind, and she urged the horse to even greater speed. They barreled onward, recklessly running a gauntlet of pitfalls. Hoofs caught a mound here, dodged a hole there, the dirt spraying outward with every strike. Still, the spirits continued to rise up left and right, shadowy wisps groping and clutching.

Suddenly the world seemed to collapse, and Liz Anne and the horse went down. Her forward momentum drove her into the animal's neck, but her bound hands kept her in the saddle even as the bay rolled to its on-side shoulder. If not for the deep seat and high swell, the force would have crushed her leg. Even as it was, she figured she was plenty bruised, for her shoulder and hip felt on fire.

The horse began to wallow, scraping her pinned leg against packed earth. The animal persisted in its attempts to rise, but even though she unwrapped her free leg from the barrel-like rib cage, her full weight still pulled against the horn. The feeble horse was just as pinned to the ground as she, here where the angels of darkness seemed to swarm.

Liz Anne closed her eyes against the horrors and prayed. But she could still hear the hoofs of skulking demons, still hear the wails of the damned in a single cry that became an eery chorus. They were calling, and soon she would join them, a fitting end for the plaything of one so evil as Perez.

"Thou shalt not be afraid for the terror by night."

The words of a psalm flashed through Liz Anne's mind like illuminated words on a page. Her father had been a man of such faith, and he had imparted to her a trust in a Higher Power. But Liz Anne knew that she was beyond help, in this life or any that might follow.

"For he shall give his angels charge over thee, to keep thee in all thy ways."

Strange, the manner in which more of that passage came to her. This time, it seemed conveyed not by thought, but by spoken word, generated by a voice so very, very familiar.

A voice that was Liz Anne's own.

With the revelation that the words came from her lips, her fears began to rush away as though swept by a mighty wind. All of a sudden, that dark nook in her mind awakened, and she opened her eyes to an abandoned prairie dog town— nothing more—and realized that the wails were but the yipping of coyotes, and the demons' hoof-beats the slow drumming of an approaching horse.

Perez!

Liz Anne figured that her mad flight had carried

her a little off trail, but that mattered little the way her bay continued to thrash. Despite the shadows, Perez would be sure to see movement off to the side, just as she could look over her shoulder toward the valley rim and discern the silhouette of rider and horse moving against the sky.

Twisting, she searched for the reins that she could never hope to reach with secured hands. A stretch of rawhide snaked along the gelding's neck and wriggled with every swing of the animal's head. She lunged, trying to seize it with her mouth, but the slithering strip eluded her efforts until she was sure Perez had already reached the valley bottom. Finally she caught it between her teeth and yanked, only to find that she had no leverage on the bit.

Tied at the wrists, she still had use of her fingers, and with her teeth she drew the relaxed rawhide to her hand. Now, at least, she could maintain a hold as she searched for that elusive leverage. Inch by inch, she worked her teeth up the rein and delivered her gains incrementally to her fingers. The painstaking process demanded that she anticipate the horse's every flail, but after the longest minute of her life, she claimed a position she might exploit.

With teeth and hands, she pulled with all her strength, forcing the bay's head back against its shoulder. Jess had told her how a rider could hold a horse flush on the ground this way—"all day long," he had said. For her purposes, though, Liz Anne hoped only to hold out long enough for Perez to ride on by.

That is, if he hadn't spied her already.

She buried her face against foamy horsehide and listened to the slow clomp of stumbling hoofs. They grew in intensity until they almost seemed on top of her, and she redoubled her efforts to keep the bay in check. But her jaws ached from the strain and her arm quivered all the way up to her shoulder, even though her fingers alone clutched rawhide.

The hoofbeats slowed even more and then stopped altogether—and Liz Anne's breaths stopped with them.

She waited for the inevitable. Any moment she would hear Perez curse and swing down from his mount. He would drag her head back by the hair, exposing her throat, and, if she were lucky, he would slide his knife edge across. She would gurgle and thrash for a few seconds, just as her father had done, but then it would be over and she would be gathered into God's arms if He would have her.

The seconds dragged on without resolution. Why didn't Perez just do it and get it over with? It was as if he was intentionally delaying, torturing her like a cat with a mouse.

Finish it! She cried silently. *Just finish it, you coward!*

She heard the strike of a hoof, followed by the beat of more hoofs—slow drumming growing quieter and quieter across the distance.

Liz Anne took her teeth from the rein and looked. Against the budding stars low in the west, death receded on a dark horse, but death was still very much all about her as well.

With her relaxed grip on the rawhide, the bay resumed its desperate struggle to rise, but as Liz Anne turned, she found the attempts as futile as ever. Somehow, she had to unshackle the animal of her weight. She tried again to loosen the knot with her teeth, but if anything, the horse wreck had only tightened it more. She tested the rope's strength, but the frayed fibers remained all too strong. Her options were running out, but if she could reach the far-side cinch, she might be able to unbuckle it and slide the saddle from the horse's withers. She didn't quite know how it would benefit her—she would still be secured to the saddle—but any chance of survival depended first on the bay gaining its feet.

Survival.

Liz Anne wanted to die, but that part of her that held Jess in her heart wanted to live, and she just didn't know which half of her was stronger.

She placed her free leg across the horse's protruding ribs and found the cinch buckle with her toe. She toyed with it blindly, hoping to work the girt free, but Perez had tightened the strap

178

only hours before and the buckle held stubbornly.

Liz Anne closed her eyes, for a minute or an hour, and when she opened them, a dozen glowing eyes stared back at her from out of the gloom.

She shrank, but there was no place to go, even when the felled horse went wild, its every effort to rise pounding her pinned leg against earth. The sets of eyes began to move, two to the left, three to the right, another pair zigzagging before her and growing larger.

She had regained enough of her senses to know these terrors by night for the wolves that they were. Maybe the hants had been products of her imagination, but the circling fangs offered an end no less horrid.

"Git! Git!" she cried, instinctively jerking at her bonds.

She looked over her shoulder and found shining eyes coming up on her flank. The wolves were on top of her, about to eat her alive. She could almost feel the hot-iron burn of their snapping jaws, could already anticipate the shredding flesh and spewing blood as those teeth would rip at her throat.

The eyes sprang at her, and she met them with a desperate kick that drove hard into cartilage and bone. To a quick yelp, the eyes retreated into the night, but there were plenty of others to take their place.

One set ventured too close to a rear hoof, and

Liz Anne rallied to the cracking of a skull. Another dark shape lunged for the horse's windpipe, but a pawing foreleg fended it off. Still, here in the valley of death's shadow, her end was certain.

Liz Anne closed her eyes, accepting what had to be, even as an image of Jess's face stirred all kinds of longing for the life she would never have.

The quick *boom! boom! boom!* of a revolver shook her into awareness. Craning, she saw two bursts of gunfire light up the night and hasten the flight of the dark shapes whose shining eyes had been upon her.

"*Quien es?*" asked a voice from out of the gloom.

"*Perez?*" called another.

Liz Anne didn't answer, for the darkness now held something far worse than it had only moments before.

FIFTEEN

Lost in the night astride a statue of a horse, Perez sat slumped over the saddle horn.

He didn't know the last time the animal had moved. Every so often, Perez had forced himself into awareness and urged the roan into a walk again, but this time he wanted only to sleep the sleep from which no one ever awoke.

180

He could have found plenty of reasons to continue blaming the girl for his misfortune, but the dazed Mexican harbored the greater anger for her father. He had been a viejo, an old man like the gringo who had raised Perez. That fact alone would have been enough to stir his rage, considering the domination and abuse he had endured as a child. But the hellcat's father had earned an extra measure of hatred for having displayed the sidesaddle so prominently in the tack house. Not only that, but the elderly Americano had taken no steps to conceal the girl when Perez had roused him in the night.

Indeed, she had peeped around the door as the viejo had stepped out on the porch with a kerosene lamp. Had Perez not seen her finely chiseled features in the flickering light, he might have figured the sidesaddle's owner for a hag as old as the viejo. Consequently, he might have ridden away without suffering all that had ensued.

Si, it was the old man's fault, his and every viejo's who had ever crossed Perez's path.

From out of the night came the sudden sound of hoofs in slow beat. Perez did his best to drift ever-deeper into oblivion, but the hoofs grew increasingly louder until they broke the bonds of his stupor. Lifting his head, he looked back up an arroyo with sculpted banks and counted three approaching riders silhouetted against the rising moon.

Perez drew his revolver as he wheeled his mount in a solid rock bed to face ally or foe. The motion of his gelding in the flooding moonlight must have caught the riders' attention, for they stopped abruptly.

Perez placed his thumb on the revolver's hammer and eased it back. If he was going to die, he wanted to do so on his own terms, not on those of whoever had opened fire when the sandstorm had struck. He kept his gaze riveted on the three as the standoff persisted, but with peripheral vision he noted a great mass looming at his right shoulder. He didn't risk a glance, but it seemed to blot out a quarter of the starry sky as might a lofty mountain.

Suddenly a shadow rider seemed to twitch, or maybe it was only in Perez's delirium, but Perez reflexively squeezed the trigger and the hammer snapped forward against an empty cartridge. His last shot had brought down the vulture, and he had forgotten to reload.

"*Quien es!*" demanded a hoarse voice.

The firing pin of Perez's six-shooter clicked futilely against another spent cartridge, then another and another. *Madre de Dios*! They would end his misery right here and now!

A pistol ball whizzed by Perez's ear to a piercing report. His horse shied, or else the slug from an ensuing rifle blast might have done more than ricochet harmlessly through the night at his back.

"Perez? *Quien es!*" cried a second voice.

Ay Dios! It was Rodriguez and Ernesto who had parted his hair with that pistol ball!

"Cabrons! Don't shoot!" Perez shouted.

He lowered his revolver, and the three shadow riders advanced from out of the swollen moon flaring orange on the horizon. As Perez watched and waited, he noticed several pools of moonlight before them in the drainage's rock bottom. Small ovals, they reflected the rising orb with all the efficiency of a looking glass.

Abruptly the horses stopped, the nose of each stretching toward its own moon fire, and Perez suddenly understood why his roan had been so affixed to this place—the drainage cradled dozens of mortar holes brimming with run-off.

Perez's cracked lips trembled. He frantically dismounted in a half-controlled fall that landed him in a heap. He didn't have the strength to scramble to his feet, but a crawl suited him fine, even as the limestone shelf brutalized his knees all the way to the nearest shimmering reflection. Sprawling on his belly, his palms on either side of the basin, he buried his face in the water.

Maria purisima! Never had anything tasted so wonderful. He gulped again and again, feeling it cool his fiery throat and race into his stomach. When he paused for air, he heard his confederates' cries of "Agua! Agua!" and he glanced over to see their dark outlines drop from their horses to seek other pockets of water. The third silhouette stayed mounted, and only now did Perez deduce the rider's identity.

He cried a warning, and from the bedrock a dark hand seized the reins just as the girl tried to goad her animal into bolting.

Perez resumed drinking, cupping water with his hand once the level dropped lower, and not until he had exhausted two basins and part of another did he roll over, bloated to the point of sickness. Moaning, he rubbed his aching belly as he writhed under the stars and that great looming shadow at his shoulder.

Finally he sat up, finding a matching shadow across from the first, two apparent mountains squeezing close. He had heard of this place where the Castle Mountains yawned, defining the two-mile-long cleft known as Castle Gap that opened on its far side to the Pecos flats. Now that they had found the gap's tinajas of water, he began to regain his confidence in spanning this no-man's land that stretched all the way to the security of Chihuahua and that rich hacienda owner waiting for a young white wife.

To reap the reward, though, he first had to protect his investment.

"The señorita," he said to his confederates, who likewise had drunk their fill. "Cut her down."

Draped across the saddle horn, she was semi-conscious at best, but the two men managed to untie her and let her slide off into their arms. Dragging her to an untapped mortar hole, they splashed water in her face until she revived enough to seek it for herself. She drank like the thirst-crazed girl she was, struggling from one tinaja to a second until she finally collapsed exhausted but hydrated.

Perez, satisfied that she was no longer in danger, crawled to his horse and used the stirrup strap to pull himself up. Taking his quirt from the horn, he stumbled over to where the girl stretched face-down. He stood over her, poking his tongue into the hole through his cheek. For a while he had been numb to the pain, lost in the hell of his thirst, but with water had come a renewed sensitivity and then unadulterated agony.

As his anger grew into rage, he quirted her across the thighs with all the force that he would have used on an unruly bronc.

She flinched and gave a sharp cry, then twisted around, her sunken cheek gleaming in the moonlight. When Perez struck her a second time, she tried to drag herself away, but he followed along, delighting in her pain as he scourged her legs.

After a half-dozen lashes, he held his arm. He wanted to punish her for her escape attempt, not injure beyond what a couple of weeks' rest in Chihuahua could fix.

"No mas!" he growled. "I'll kill you like I did the old gringo!"

The girl was moaning as she stretched the back of her hand to her thigh, but as she turned her head, Perez could still read defiance in her face.

"Animal," she whispered. "Jess and the boys will track you to perdition."

"Que?"

"I'll be dead, but they'll make you pay."

"Jess and muchachos," mused Perez. "Vaqueros?"

"They won't ever give up, you coward."

So was that who had fired upon him so many miles back? Were they the reason his third confederate had disappeared in that black blizzard? More importantly, were they indeed still back there in the dark, hell-bent on riding him down and exacting vengeance, just when he seemed home free?

Perez shuddered and checked the rising moon. This very instant those vaqueros could have their sights trained on him, ready to put a bullet between his eyes. And if they didn't, what assurance did he have that they wouldn't overtake him sooner or later, just as the girl had said? For the rest of his life, he might have to look over his shoulder, wondering and fearing.

Perez turned to the slope, a battleground of massive boulders and fortress-like rim rock taking form in the moonlight. The vaqueros' horses would smell water and carry them to this very spot, just as the roan had brought Perez, and he would be lying in wait above to end the chase once and for all.

Perez smiled a devil's smile. "This Jess, his vaqueros," he said to the girl. "I want to meet those cabrons. Get up!"

All through the long, desperate night, Sarah seemed to walk at Tom's side, a wisp of flowing moonlight both reassuring and troubling on this trail of death. She was alive again, at least in his dreams, and from her he drew strength and even hope. Yet he was denied the very thing that he longed for most—to pull her close and beg forgiveness. He reached for her time and again, but she always remained just beyond his touch, no matter how much he strained.

Sarah!

Sarah!

Why wouldn't she melt into his arms and accept all that his heart had to say? Was it because her head slumped to the side and her face held a bloody rivulet? Couldn't she find it in her soul to forgive, even if he could never forgive himself?

The brush of something against his leg stirred Tom to the here and now. He and Dee were astride a horse as he opened his eyes, and past the boy's shoulder Tom could see their exaggerated shadows preceding them down a canyon drainage illuminated by early morning sunlight. Pulling ahead at close quarters was an appaloosa with Sorrels in the saddle, and the animated rider seemed bent on attaining some nearby goal. Tom's own horse also seemed to move with purpose now, after so many hours of creeping along mechanically.

For forty yards four sets of hoofs beat out a cadence against a solid rock bed, then Sorrels dropped awkwardly from the saddle and began to scramble forward on all fours.

What in the hell . . .

Down past his own mount's nodding head, Tom saw sky reflecting in dozens of small pools and understood. It was water—not mud or blood or urine—but honest-to-God water!

"Young fellow, young fellow," Tom rasped, gently shaking the boy and reining up.

"Good Lord! Good Lord!"

Tom didn't know if the hoarse cry came from Jess or Gabe, but both were suddenly abreast and spilling from their horses. Tom glanced over, knowing he needed help with Dee if not for himself, and was not surprised to see Jess refuse a watery mortar hole at the hoofs of his mount in order to lend a hand. Gabe had already dropped to his knees at a basin, only to look over at Tom guiltily and stumble to their aid without drinking. Sorrels alone ignored their plight and plopped belly-down to immerse his face in a pool.

Tom passed the boy down into their waiting arms, only to find himself frozen to his horse. Even now, Tom wouldn't say a word as he struggled in vain to peel himself from the saddle, but as soon as the 7L hands had Dee on the bedrock, Jess came around and slipped Tom's right foot from the stirrup. Tom's legs had all but lost feeling, but the wagon boss worked from both sides of the saddle and finally got him down. For a man like Tom, who had always prided himself in self-sufficiency in everything except matters of the heart, it was a damned sorry situation.

But he didn't have long to dwell on it. A rifle shot rang out and rock exploded at his feet. He whirled to the close-set mountain at his left shoulder, a steep slope of massive boulders, cacti, and junipers. Rising hundreds of feet to rim rock riddled with dark overhangs, it was a twin to a slightly more distant mountain that loomed over a knoll on the opposite side of the gulch.

The report rolled through the pass, playing between the sister mesas. Tom spun with the reverberation, instinctively trying to pinpoint its source, then arms stronger than his own tugged at him.

"Get down!" cried Jess.

Tom dropped flat to the *pop! pop! pop!* of a volley that kicked up more shards of rock. The deceptive echo and the way the bullets struck and sang and struck again made it seem as if they were under attack by a whole army. But every firearm had a distinctive report, and Tom distinguished only a single rifle and two revolvers. Still, in a place made-to-order for ambush, he knew that three guns were two more than anybody needed.

For a split-second Jess's horse was between Tom and the snipers, then the animal boogered and left Tom staring up at three puffs of smoke in a jumble of boulders on the left-side mountain's lower slope. But Tom wasn't just looking and counting and waiting for a bullet with his name on it—he was belly-crawling straight into the gunfire. If he could reach the sharp drainage bank that lay on a direct line down from the shooters, he would have a defensible position from which to fight back.

To do so, though, he had to pass over the very pools for which body and soul had screamed for so many days now. Water splashed his cheek as he gripped a basin for leverage, but he felt the sting of flying rock as well. He had to have water, had to stop and plunge his face into a pool, but all he could do was let basin after basin drag wet across his torso as he kept up his snake-track slither through dancing bullets. If ever there was maddening torture, this was it.

A quick bursting of rock lifted Tom's boot off the ground, then he was under the four-foot bank and catching falling rubble on his hat brim. He thought he was hit, but as he dragged his leg to cover, he saw only a fresh crease in the leather above his boot heel.

Tom drew himself up against the dirt breast-work and reconnoitered the heights. He must have popped up prairie dog-like a little too much, for something fanned his hair and his hat flew off.

The SOBs! They were peppering him head to toe, and if he wasn't careful, they would find his sweet spot and end it all right there!

He reached cross-body for his .44 and came up empty. Hell! He turned to the drainage and found Jess and Gabe dragging Dee by the shoulders in his direction. They were stumbling and dodging bullets, and Tom didn't have so much as a slingshot to lay down cover fire.

"My gun!" he shouted to Jess.

The thought must have already occurred to the wagon boss, for he had already whipped out one of the three revolvers in his waistband and was sliding it across rock toward Tom. Tom lunged into the open, hearing the whiz of another ricochet, and came up with Dee's .45. Risking life that he no longer held precious, he twisted around to the puffs of smoke far up past the bank's rim and opened up.

It took only two quick shots to quell the shooters' fire, but he squeezed off another two rounds to ensure that the 7L hands made it to cover.

"Young fellow all right?" he cried, throwing himself against the bank.

Safe now at Tom's side, Jess was already running a hand down the kid's frame in search. "Don't see no blood!" He lifted his gaze. "You all right, Tom?"

Tom trembled with a weakness that not even adrenalin could overcome. "Where's that Winchester of ours? Revolver can't reach 'em!"

Tom and Jess both looked at Gabe, who shook his head. "Still on the paint with my scatter gun! They was shootin' at me same's they was y'all!"

Jess turned back to the mountain beyond the sloughed bank. "Damned sure got us pinned down! How many you think?"

"For God's sake, give me a gun!"

Tom leaned out just far enough to look around Jess's shoulder. Gabe's floppy hat still partially blocked his view, but he saw all he needed. Fifteen yards down the drainage, Sorrels cowered under the bank.

Tom exchanged glances with Jess. There were a lot of questions in the young man's sunburned eyes, and Tom knew they all had to do with the .45 he now gripped.

"Whatever it is between y'all," said Jess, "this ain't the time. My Lord, Tom, have we caught 'em? They got Liz Anne up there somewhere?" The 7L hand suddenly paled. "Good God, can we risk shootin' back?"

"Can't just sit here like it's a turkey shoot and we're the turkeys!" interjected Gabe. "Gotta have that rifle! Looka yonder—ol' paint done took a step toward Sorrels."

"I don't want him with a gun in his hand when Liz Anne might be there!" exclaimed Jess. "He done tried to be a hero once and could've got her killed!"

Gabe gave Jess a hard look. "You ain't been thinkin' clear ever since they dragged that little girl off. Thing is, if we don't have somethin' to show 'em we mean business, we's all gonna be dead. And they don't have to shoot a one of us to do it—all they gotta do is keep us from them water holes and let that sun get a little higher."

Tom could see deliberation in every crease of Jess's face as the wagon boss turned to him.

"I expect," said Tom, not waiting to be asked his opinion, "you know the answer for yourself."

Jess winced and turned away with a wag of his head. "Damned if I know anything anymore. All I know's Liz Anne's maybe a stone's throw away and I'm squattin' here like some kind of coward."

"You're lots of things, son," said Tom, "but a coward you ain't."

"Damned fool is what he is," Gabe mumbled under his breath.

Jess went red and whirled on him. "What the hell's got in to you, Gabe? We been like brothers, and here you've turned into the biggest pile of—"

"He's scared, son," interrupted Tom. "He know's he's dyin' and he's plum' scared to death. He's hoorawed his way through things too long and he don't know how to handle it."

"You damned tootin'," admitted Gabe. "I'm an ol' scared-y cat that's done used up eight of his

193

lives and is hangin' on to that ninth one by a whisker. Don't tell me y'all don't feel no different either."

"Maybe I'm dyin', all right, Gabe," said Jess, "but I'm too busy tryin' to get Liz Anne back to worry about it. I figure my life for hers is a fair trade."

"Yeah, well, just remember you ain't got the right to go swap anybody's life but your own."

Gabe didn't waste another breath. He turned to Sorrels with words too quiet for the shooters to hear.

"Sorrels! Grab hold of that rifle!"

Embracing the bank, a forearm protecting his skull, Sorrels allowed himself only a glance in Gabe's direction.

"The paint!" Gabe continued. "Behind you there! We gotta have that Winchester or they'll be singin' hymns over us!"

Sorrels looked over his shoulder. On bullet-scarred rock twenty feet behind him, the horse stood drinking from a mortar hole.

"I'll get my damned head blowed off!" he contended.

"You got a better chance than any of us!" spoke up Jess. "We gotta slow down their fire so we can get to that water!"

"Why the hell should I go riskin' my life for any of you?"

"Then do it for yourself!" countered Jess.

194

Gabe turned to Jess and Tom. "He don't need water the way we do. He's the only one got a drink while ago."

Jess glanced up at the bank. "How many you count, Tom?"

"Three of 'em. Two six-shooters and a rifle."

Jess looked down at Dee. "He's gotta have drink, I tell you. I figure those Mexes done watered up."

"You can bet your bottom dollar on it, son."

Jess passed a hand along the unconscious boy's forehead and then studied the arroyo past Sorrels. "Suppose a man could work his way down-canyon huggin' the bank? If they don't see me, I might be able to break out on top, circle up behind the murderin' devils."

Tom considered every aspect of Jess's features—the firm, bristly jaw, the dirt-defined lines of determination in his forehead, the eyes that burned steely in more ways than one. Everything about him spoke of the same bulldog tenacity that Tom had found in himself at those adobe walls. He knew all too well that courage and unflagging resolve weren't always enough to save the woman of a man's heart, but he admired this young man more than he could say. If the two of them had only been together that night at Horsehead Crossing . . .

"Son," Tom told him, "I just ain't able to go with you or I would."

"I know it, Tom." Jess looked at Gabe, and Tom saw that for a moment their gazes locked. Then

Gabe's eyes dropped in a manner that spoke volumes.

Jess's chest expanded and he slipped across Dee and began edging past Gabe.

"Jess, I—"

At the sound of Gabe's voice, Jess looked around and hesitated, as if he expected more words to follow. But Gabe only lowered his head and fell silent.

"Just take care of Dee," Jess told him, and then he was gone, creeping against the shielding bank.

SIXTEEN

Jess expected his next confrontation to be with those Mexicans, but just as he tried to slip past Sorrels without showing himself to the shooters, the unarmed man lunged for Tom's .44 in his waistband.

Just in time, Jess slapped a hand to the grip. "Leave it!" he whispered.

"Why the hell can't I? Naked as a jaybird and you got one for each hand!"

"That's the way it's gonna stay, too."

Jess stepped across Sorrels's legs and started away.

"I'll see you in hell!" snapped Sorrels.

Jess paused. "Figure you already made your bed there. You might as well lay in it."

In a near daze, Jess crept on, scraping the crumbling bank to avoid a bullet. His motor skills were so impaired that he repeatedly dropped to a hand or knee, but worse was the self-doubt that assailed him. Maybe Gabe was right. Maybe he was a damned fool in some ways, especially in thinking he could climb that mountain. Even if by some miracle he succeeded, would he have the strength left to raise a revolver?

He was more dead than not, but Liz Anne's face lived stronger than ever in his mind.

Sporadic gunfire continued, but since dirt never flew from the bank's rim and no ricochet screamed down the gulch, he figured he hadn't given himself away. Stealth and guile, however, could carry him only so far in face of weakness so intense that every step was a challenge.

Everything began to whirl and he fell again, and this time he lay panting with eyes closed and cheek against rock and felt himself drifting away. He had forced himself to the brink and beyond, but every man had his limit, even if driven by a cause greater than self.

He wished he could die at peace, but he couldn't erase the haunting regrets. There was that awful scene through the cracked shed wall, and there was an even darker one, if possible, in his imagination—a graphic picture of innocence and purity overwhelmed by the lowest sons of hell.

Jess was not a church-going man—few cowhands were—and he supposed that he had strayed a lot since his mother had sat him down with a dog-eared Bible and taught him to read. But for the first time since his father had died, a prayer passed his lips.

He persisted in the whisper as the world disappeared in dark oblivion and he began to yield to a sleep from which he would never awaken. But with a will that seemed to draw strength from somewhere else, he forced his eyes open one last time.

The bedrock unfurled in a blur to a strange pocket of sky so close that he was almost in it. Maybe it was the clouds of Heaven opening, or, more likely, judgment teasing him with a lie. Still, he stretched out an arm, straining to reach this glimpse into things beyond a simple cowboy's life.

His quaking fingers inched closer and then they were there, sharing in a sky that stimulated his sense of touch. Withdrawing, he brought his hand to lips as cracked as old saddle leather and tasted wetness.

It was a pool of water that mirrored the sky—blessed water for which he had combed this hell on earth for mile after terrible mile.

Dragging himself closer, he plunged his face into the tinaja. He drank madly, gulping and gagging and pausing only long enough to breathe. Even as his stomach knotted, water continued to stream down his throat in answer to a drawn body still screaming for it. Finally he had downed all he could, and he rested his cheek on shady rock and felt the racing of a heart that had seemed only a few beats from pumping its last.

Time was vital in so many ways. With every passing minute, the sun would rise higher, increasing the likelihood that his companions wouldn't get out of that arroyo alive. Any second, those Mexicans might tire of the fight and flee on horses that had watered and rested. And this very instant Liz Anne might be surrendering the one thing that could carry a person when nothing else would—hope.

Jess knew all these things, but even will and courage couldn't overcome the limitations of a body unable to take another step. He began to fade into unconsciousness, and he fought it all the way to the point at which his eyes rolled up into their sockets.

He awoke not knowing if he had been asleep for seconds or hours, but the shadow that had given him respite was now a thin line under the casting bank and the sun beat down on his exposed cheek. Plenty of time had passed, all right. But a quick exchange of revolver fire told him there was still life in the arroyo and a presence up in those boulders, critical emotional lifts that buoyed the strength that had returned a little with water and rest.

Jess saw that he lay at the mouth of a dark side

drainage, a miniature defile with sharp walls of alkali a few feet high. Its bed, eighteen inches wide, extended muddy for several yards to a pair of foot-high rock ledges stairstepping up. Past this pour-off, the hewn channel threaded onward before bending out of sight—a way to steal closer to those maggots who had Liz Anne.

Jess worked his way inside and inched forward, his shoulders scraping the banks. It was as if he crawled through a freshly dug grave, the tumbling rubble like a live burial. He bellied up across the pour-off and slithered around the bend to find the channel twisting back in an S. The sinuous passage grew increasingly steep as he forged on, negotiating mud and gravel and additional pour-offs. Then the gully tightened even more, forcing Jess to squeeze through sideways, and finally he had no choice but to get his feet under him.

The banks were neck-high here, and he had his finger on the trigger as he peered out over the barrel of his .41. Before him was the ocher face of a great, lichen-covered boulder, partially wreathed by catclaw and prickly pear. Checking the slope below, he was surprised to learn that he had gained considerable elevation. But as he swung the revolver left to right across the boulder, and on toward the recessed head of a steep side canyon studded with cedars, he found a lot of imposing mountain still above. It rose hundreds of feet, and he set his sights on the white-washed rim rock below a summit ridge stark against sky and began to climb.

He broke around the massive rock only to find others still muffling the sound of rifle fire. He took it as good fortune, for what he couldn't see couldn't spot him either. When he was past the boulders and only cacti and shrubs flanked him, he slipped the revolver back in his waistband and crept on all fours, a position that the severe incline virtually demanded anyway.

As sharp talus grated his hands, a mist clouded his vision. Wiping his brow into his sleeve, he realized that he sweated for the first time since far back up-trail. The water was doing its job, all right; now if he could only do his.

His lungs heaved as he weakened, forcing him to stop and struggle for air. He went on that way, advancing and pausing, his tortured chest and aching legs stripping away his will. He caught tasajillo and prickly pear in his arms and legs, but the lechuguilla was the worst, a shin-high gauntlet of clumped knives too extensive to dodge. Finally will and body both abandoned him at once, and he collapsed to the agonizing pierce of stilettos.

Dizzy and breathless, the sun like hellfire against his back, Jess wondered if this was how it would end—a coward surrendering when he might be so close.

Like hell! He would fight to the last!

It took him a half-minute of futility to rise again,

201

but once there he focused only on the next step, and the one after that. In his daze he seemed to crawl up out of a great, dark pit intent on dragging him back. Then his hat struck something hard, and he stopped and stretched a hand up against a lichen-painted wall of limestone that ended at sky far above.

Jess looked left and right, finding the cliff intimidating except where great sections had collapsed. Turning into a stiff wind, he experienced vertigo at the sight of the main canyon falling away three hundred feet to a twisting maze of arroyos punctuated by buttes. On across, three-quarters of a mile maybe, another rock-rimmed mesa shared in defining a gap more rugged than anything Jess had ever seen.

The muted sound of a rifle drew his attention to a boulder field back up-canyon and two-thirds down the slope under his boots. Ever since he had gained the cliff's base, he had steadied himself with a hand against rock, but now he pulled his pearl-handled .41 with his right hand and Tom's .44 with his left—two deadly agents of judgment.

Hugging the rim rock, Jess worked his way toward a position directly above those vermin who had so much judgment coming to them.

He stumbled across wobbly stones and skirted dark overhangs large and small. Before one stirrup-shaped opening, he almost stepped on a six-foot rattlesnake stretched out in the sun.

Mounting a knee-high rock at the head of a treacherous landslide chute, he heard another *crack!* of the rifle from down and away, where patina-darkened boulders blocked the lower reaches. Then his footing gave way, and suddenly Jess was down on his hip and the small boulder that had been underfoot was rolling down the mountain.

It picked up speed and force and carried more rocks with it, a small landslide thundering and throwing a terrible dust into the wind. Jess could feel the destruction telegraphed all the way up to where he lay. The whole mountain seemed ready to collapse, and he scrambled for safety like a crippled dog.

He dislodged more rocks but reached solid ground across the chute without the slide carrying him away. Shaken, he lay wheezing in the boiling dust as the rumble grew fainter and then ended.

He came to his feet and found the gray-white cloud dissipating, revealing the ghosts of the boulders below. Then sunlight glinted from the haze, and a rock at Jess's boot exploded.

Jess danced an awkward step to the gunshot's echo. They'd spotted him! The slide had alerted them to the heights, and now he was fodder for that big gun of theirs!

He spun to the rim as another *boom!* fragmented rock. A dozen feet up the slope was a horizontal slit of black, a dreadful grimace in the rim rock's base. The overhang was twenty feet wide, and at the midway point a wiry, three-foot column joined floor and ceiling just inside.

Jess bolted for it with a frantic first step that was too ambitious for his battered legs. He went down, the rifle slugs peppering the slope left and right, but his devotion to Liz Anne kept his boots churning. He scratched his way on up, and just as rock shrapnel stung his cheek he dived into shadows thick with a cave's musty smell.

The bullets followed him in, ricocheting in the gloom. He recoiled from a sharp pain at his eyebrow—a grazing slug perhaps—and rolled deeper. Maybe the place swarmed with rattlers and maybe it didn't, but there was certain death at the entrance's twilight.

He heard telltale maracas, but the relentless gunfire concerned him more, driving him to cover behind the willowy column. Weather-worn and crumbling, it gave the illusion of supporting the mighty shelf above.

Illusion.

As the bullets chipped away at the fragile silhouette, Jess could only wait for the rattler's strike and wonder.

His time for pondering was short. Simultaneous with a rifle's report, more rock branded his face, and for an instant bright sky showed through a six-inch separation in the pillar. Then the entire mountain groaned ominously and the gap was gone, the overhead tons dropping and then hesitating, stayed for the moment by a column now a half-foot shorter.

As rubble rained down, Jess weighed his chances. *Inside or out.*

He chose out, rifle fire and all, but never had time to act. To a roar greater than any thunder, the column gave way, the overhanging shelf crashing down with it.

There was smothering dust and abrupt darkness and a rumble that didn't want to end. Jess coughed and wheezed, choked by a cloud he couldn't see, but he could still feel plenty. Something hard and heavy pinned his chest and legs, a limestone vice determined to squeeze the life from him.

Maybe the quicker to die the better, but Jess's instinct for survival overwhelmed any rational analysis. He cried out, driven by panic, and began a fight for escape that he knew he couldn't win.

Rubble still fell as he wriggled an arm into the open, finding he still gripped the .41. He threw it aside and swept rock after rock from his torso. Then he loosed his other arm, along with a second revolver that he discarded, and at least he was free to die with his hands in a backslidden cowboy's prayer. It was the only way for this to end, for his legs seemed hopelessly trapped under an angling shelf of black hell.

Jess had heard of one woman who would have been buried alive if not for crying out from the coffin at her very grave. The only difference with Jess was that nobody would hear.

He wondered which would come first, insanity or death, but while he wondered, he struggled. He battled for minutes or hours; it was all the same in this timeless purgatory where he paid penance for failing Liz Anne and his father.

As his eyes adjusted, he detected faint glows at two extremes—the collapsed entrance and the cave depths. That meant fresh air, which also raised the prospect of suffering for days before he died. But as exhaustion forced him to relax his muscles, he found that by twisting his hips, his legs were no longer locked in place. Before, he had been without hope; now, a mere wisp of it gave him new life.

He began to squirm and push in opposition to the immovable shelf across his pelvis. He inched out a little at a time as rock gnawed at his thighs, knees, shins. He was like a snake shedding its skin, and just when he thought he was pinned again as hopelessly as ever, he suddenly was free.

Free. Did a man with six feet of dirt over him have the right to think in those terms?

But judging by touch this grave had squeeze ways, and after groping for and finding the six-shooters, Jess belly-crawled through a debris maze and came up before a keyhole of light where the entrance had been. He could fit only a single digit inside, but for the first time he began to believe he might get out of this alive.

As soon as he began to dig, reality dashed his spirits again. These weren't rocks that a man could remove one at a time, but massive, slanted shelves that a team of horses seemed unlikely to dislodge. But at least a draft of air in his face confirmed a second opening somewhere, maybe back at that other glow in the depths.

First, though, Jess had to exhaust possibilities here. He tested the blockage again to the patter of falling dirt, but went silent when he heard voices. Pressing his eye to the keyhole, he looked through in the same way that he had at that shed as an eight-year-old.

This time, it wasn't his despondent father he saw, but a shrivel-armed Mexican dragging a haggard young woman up the mountain.

Liz Anne!

She was in his field of vision for only an instant, but it was long enough for Jess to read the hopelessness in her blistered face and to hear a couple of Spanish words from offstage.

Caballos. Mesa.

Then she and her captors were gone, their legs taking them up over the very keyhole through which Jess peered.

He wanted to cry out, to encourage Liz Anne to keep up hope, but he realized it would only alert the Mexicans to the fact that he was alive. For all

Jess knew, his companions were dead, leaving the element of surprise his only ally if he ever escaped this damnable hole.

Twisting around, he frantically squirmed back through the maze and again detected a faint glow deeper in the mountain. But reaching it was another matter, even if the cave-in had silenced the rattler.

He repeatedly banged his skull as he negotiated squeeze ways, clambered over rubble, wormed through places so tight that it peeled his hide. But finally he came to the bottom of a twilight-bathed chimney with boulders rising in a jumble to a slot of daylight eighty feet above.

Jess hesitated only long enough to steel himself for a climb that no man so tortured had any business trying. Coming to his feet, he found a handhold and began dragging himself up.

He climbed only a yard before his boot slipped and he fell, a crumpled heap with nothing left but will and an image of Liz Anne that refused to let him give up.

Unfolding himself, he again squirmed up through a well that, after the first few feet, bear-hugged him so tightly that even a slipping boot wasn't much of a factor. He could hear his heart drumming like hoofs, his chest laboring like a winded horse at full gallop. He paid dearly for every vertical inch, his entire body screaming *No more! No more!*

Soon, every step higher demanded a full minute's rest, then two minutes, three. He could climb no faster, even as he realized that, prior to the ambush, the Mexicans must have led their caballos to the summit through a break in the rim rock. By now, they must have long since reached the staked animals and taken flight with a girl who deserved so much more than Jess was able to give.

All the way up, he climbed with visceral grunts, but he forced himself to silence as he came to an overhead slit of jagged daylight a little too small for his shoulders.

Removing his hat, he popped through just far enough for the brightness to blind him. Squinting, he found himself in the shade of a modest boulder a few feet away. He scanned his surroundings, learning that he was in a shallow sinkhole on the mesa summit. The sink's rock-lined rim was only a yard high, but it was lofty enough to block his view of the tableland.

Jess grew still, listening for secrets his vision couldn't tell him. He heard the rush of the wind, the call of a chaparral, his own heaving breaths —and nothing more.

Dropping back inside, he slipped his arms up through the crevice in advance of his head. He managed to hang his left forearm and right wrist across the lip, but even after scrunching his shoulders, he couldn't drag himself through.

Again Jess retreated, and as he rested he

inspected the slit from below. It was defined for the most part by solid limestone, but an area at four o'clock showed a thin break.

Jess first tried to loosen the rock with his hands, but when that failed he dug into the fracture with his pocketknife. When he thought he had made headway, he again tested the area, only to fall back in frustrating exhaustion. He persisted for futile minutes—gouging, pulling, sinking—before the stone finally began to give. Still, long minutes of terrible doubt passed before he dragged a small avalanche down upon him.

Jess ducked, catching most of the rubble on his hat, but the primary rock glanced off his thigh on its way to the depths. Now the sky showed larger, enough so that he laid his revolvers on the lip and succeeded in wriggling through. The shape of the entrance demanded a half-twist of his body, leaving him facing the dead limbs of a scrub mesquite twenty-five yards away at the brink of the partially collapsed cliff.

Jess came to a cautious crouch, a gun in each hand, and slowly straightened as he swung around with the angling wind. To the east, a broken line of scrub brush fronted the rim. Past the adjacent boulder marking south unfurled a sterile plain so flat that he wondered if a raindrop would know which way to go after it fell. To the west lay more of the same—a rocky, windswept tableland sentineled by desert succulents—

except where a smudge of gray-brown hugged the earth.

The blight was lowest on the upwind side, but it rose like range fire smoke as it drifted with the currents. On a drouth-ravaged mesa such as this, the plume could mean only one thing: the dust of those Mexican riders fleeing with Liz Anne.

Once again, Jess just felt so damned helpless. He mounted the boulder, his jaw tightening as he squinted into the distance and watched the riders drop off the mesa's far side. Minutes ago, Liz Anne had been an arm's length away, and now she was fading into the horizon, a mere speck in an awful wilderness that stretched to the Pecos and far beyond. It was a dead man's river, they said, a place that even an upright man like Buckalew had always cursed.

"I figure when a bad man dies," Buckalew had commented, "he goes one of two places—to hell or the Pecos."

Theological matters may have been out of a cowboy's realm, but Jess was sure about one thing. He had a rendezvous on that damnable stream with a den of serpents too evil for even hell.

SEVENTEEN

✿ After a roar unlike anything Tom had ever heard, the canyon had gone silent but Dee had not.

Pinned down at Tom's side in the arroyo, the boy moaned in delirium, his cracked lips whispering again and again for water. Tom glanced at the pools, finding them so damned close and yet so far. But there was nothing distant about the sun, burning its way across the sky and robbing them of the bank's shade. It was death itself that stared down at this innocent kid who had sacrificed himself to those wolves, and Tom owed him too much to let him die like a sick dog.

Slipping his hat over his revolver barrel, Tom edged it over the embankment to bait the shooters into firing if they were still up there.

Nothing.

He bobbed the hat a little, trying to draw attention, but the canyon kept up its silence except for a whistling wind.

Tom had to take a chance. Maybe those butchers were just trying to lure them into the open, but at this stage it didn't make much difference anymore.

Pulling himself up with the aid of the bank, he took hat in hand and started for the basins.

"They'll bob your head!" warned Gabe.

"Hell, let the damned fool go," said Sorrels.

"Tom! Tom!" Gabe called after him in a whisper.

But Tom was on a mission, and not for himself. He stumbled into the open, wondering if he would hear the gunshot before he died—

and wondered the same thing about Sarah.

Sarah!

How could he have done it? Even believing that the unspeakable had been about to happen to her at the hands of those devils from hell, how could he have put that muzzle to her temple and—

Suddenly Tom was there, dropping before the nearest pool, the rock surging up to punish his knees and forearm. Every fiber in his body cried for drink, but Dee's drawn features screamed for it more. With his palm, Tom scooped ounce after ounce into his hat until it could hold no more. But now he was down and didn't have the strength to get up, and all he could do was turn to Dee and start crawling, dragging his leaking hat along the bedrock.

Then a shadow was in his face, and a pair of hands swept the hat up and sloshed a little across the brim.

"Got it from here, old-timer!" rasped Gabe.

Tom sank to the scorching rock and watched

Gabe stumble back to Dee. Even then, Tom refused to seek drink for himself until he could be assured that the boy would be taken care of. But that didn't stop Sorrels. As soon as Tom's gamble established that it was safe, Sorrels reeled across the arroyo and half-fell before a nearly overflowing basin.

Meanwhile, Gabe had reached the teenager to hover and tilt the hat, directing a trickle between the barely responsive lips.

"That's it, that's it, Dee," Gabe encouraged. "Sweet as milk squirtin' out of the ol' cow's teat."

Satisfied that he had done all he could for the kid, Tom crawled back for a water hole and sprawled belly-down before a full basin. Submerging his mouth and cheeks, he drank with hurried swallows as if expecting someone to snatch away this small pool of Eden. As wonderful as it was to feel wetness pouring down inside, the cool salve against his cooked face was even better.

The abrupt rumble of a rock rolling down the mountain brought him twisting about with revolver in hand. Something was up there, damned close, but Tom was looking into a blinding sun.

"It's me—I'm comin' in! You hear me? I'm comin' in!"

At the first word, Tom came within an eyelash of reflexively shooting, but he was mighty glad he hadn't when he recognized Jess's voice. Shading his eyes with his hand, Tom watched the 7L boss stumble on down and drop into the arroyo.

"We gotta get our horses!" Jess exclaimed breathlessly. "I saw her! Had their mounts waitin' on top, took off across the mountain with her!"

"What happened up there?" asked Tom. "Sounded like—"

"Dropped off the west side! Come on! Who's ridin' with me?"

From a sitting position, Tom rocked forward and shifted his weight to a supporting hand. Twice more he made futile attempts to rise, before Jess came over and helped him up.

Tom looked down the arroyo at the bags of bones that were now their horses. Normally an unsecured bronc on open range would be the devil to catch, but these broken-down animals hadn't strayed ten yards from water, even with enough gunfire and landslides to rattle the dead.

As Tom turned back to Jess, he admired again this young man's gumption, if not his common sense.

"Son," Tom said compassionately, "dead men can't help that girl none."

Jess's voice cracked. "But I saw her face, Tom. She—I could see—just hopelessness—that's all that was in her eyes!"

Tom laid a fatherly hand on Jess's shoulder. "I know. I know it's awful what them red devils done to her."

Tom was back on the Pecos, waiting for that last charge with Sarah at his side and a couple of loads in his Colt. Then the wagon boss's reciprocal hand on his shoulder dragged him out of one nightmare into another.

"These are Mexes, Tom, remember? Mexes that've got Liz Anne!"

Now Tom was clear-headed again, as clear as a man one step ahead of the undertaker could be. "Even waterin' up here and restin' a bit, they wore them horses out again crossin' that mountain."

"Their dust was still risin' in the west when I started down! Isn't Horsehead—"

"Dozen miles to that hell-hole."

"Let's go, Tom! We gotta go!"

"Maybe some salt grass on the banks. They'll be lookin' to find them horses of theirs some forage."

"Come on! We—"

"Easy, son," Tom interrupted. "They ain't goin' but twelve miles, is all. If they don't rest and graze at the river, they'll be a-walkin' here on out. We play this smart and they'll be a-waitin' there."

"Let's ride, Tom!" Jess pleaded.

"You ain't listenin'. We ain't got the men or horses. We sure 'nough gotta have both."

"So we're just gonna—"

"Damn it, Jess!"

Both of them turned to the arroyo bank, where Gabe still tended the writhing teenager.

"Just take a look at Dee, why don't you?" Gabe railed on. "Look at the way he's sufferin' and tell me you still ain't got no idea what Tom's sayin'! We gotta have rest, damn it, rest!"

For a while, Jess just stared at Gabe, then he looked away and seemed to study the horses. Tom looked the remuda over again too, and this time it was an even uglier picture than before. Finally he heard a sigh of resignation pass the wagon boss's lips.

"Soon's we're able," said Jess, "let's drag the saddles off and get those broncs staked out."

Water and shade, food and rest.

Tom knew that the four were indispensable in a mid-summer chase across this fringe of the Chihuahuan Desert, and three of them were at hand. Nourishment, however, still proved elusive for men and horses alike. Then Jess located a patch of mesquite grass in a brief hollow up out of the arroyo, and as soon as the horses were staked, Gabe brought down a pair of scrawny jackrabbits with his scatter gun. Jess added a third, and soon the hares were roasting over a scrub brush fire.

Tom's innards had gone so long without food that he had to force down the first bites, but things came easier after that. Still, the meat was tougher than old boot leather, and he swallowed whole what he couldn't chew. He ate and drank until he was bloated, and no sooner had he belched than he felt a little strength returning to his jittery frame.

Dee, though, was still a worrisome matter. With a few ounces of water poured down him, the kid stirred ever so little, and when the aroma of the roasting meat wafted his way he even made a weak gesture toward the cooking fire. They sat him up, and in a team effort, Jess supported his shoulders while Tom sliced a bite-sized piece and passed it to Gabe, who in turn slipped it between the teenager's lips.

But Dee only gagged, and Gabe dug the meat out with his fingers to keep him from choking. As the boy lapsed into unconsciousness again, all Tom could do was help make him as comfortable as possible in the tenuous shade of a scrub mesquite near the horses—that, and regret again the sacrifice that had demanded so much of this homeless waif.

While Gabe and Sorrels retreated sullenly to a mott of stunted hackberry trees beyond the animals, Tom and Jess sat under an algerita bush close to Dee, even though the fluttering leaves scarcely cast enough shade for a single person. Tom stared at the boy, whose chest rose and fell in labored rhythm.

"Got a bad feelin' about the young fellow," he said quietly.

"He's sure in a bad way, Tom. I . . ." The words seemed to choke Jess for a moment. "So many awful things are happenin', I just don't know how I'd keep goin' if it wasn't for thinkin' about Liz Anne and me. Down the road, you know."

"I know she means a lot to you, son."

Tom heard a sob hang in Jess's throat, but he allowed the 7L hand his privacy and didn't look around.

"I-I'm gonna marry her, Tom—if she'll have me."

Now Tom did face the younger man. "She'll have you. Be proud to have you. I'd've been proud if my own son had lived to be like you."

Suddenly Jess's eyes held all kinds of questions. "You say son? Did he—you know, at the river, the Indians?"

Tom's cheek twitched at the terrible memories. "Never had the chance to be borned. Guess I'll be seein' him too, soon's we get that girl back."

Jess's gaze grew so piercing that Tom had to avert his eyes.

"You're not talkin' about payin' respects at a grave, are you, Tom."

Tom turned his face to the west, for his soul was abruptly there, crushed by those falling mud walls.

"Tom, you don't want to do that," added Jess. "My Lord, Tom, don't—just don't."

Tom had never heard Jess so troubled, not even when he spoke of Liz Anne. Still, he couldn't bring himself to turn back to him.

"It's time, son. Time I made peace for pullin' that trigger."

Jess's abrupt hand on his shoulder failed to bring Tom back from that horrid night.

"What are you tellin' me?" pressed Jess. "You sayin' you . . ."

Now Tom did face him, through a blurry world—faced him to bare a soul as dark as the pits of perdition.

"They was gonna take her," Tom whispered. "Them red devils, they was gonna tear her clothes off of her and—"

Tom flinched at a stabbing pain in his chest, but he went on. "Saved my last two pistol balls, then I just had the one for me. 'Fore I could use it, freighters come up, scattered them Comanches."

"Lord, Tom. You . . . You sayin' you didn't have to—"

"Can't even remember it all, but she's still—oh son, how could I have ever—she's still just as . . ."

He never found the last word as his eyes welled and he hung his head. In a way he couldn't understand, he was glad that the younger man's hand lingered on his shoulder.

"You couldn't've knowed," managed an almost equally distraught Jess. "You just couldn't've knowed."

"Don't make it no easier. Don't mean I had a right not to use that last ball. I just rode away and kept ridin' for twenty years, knowin' what I had comin' to me. I get to Horsehead Crossin', rescue that girl, I ain't ridin' no more."

Tom turned away and fell silent, but no more silent than this young cowhand who had come to mean so much to him. When Jess's voice finally sounded again, it carried a plea more fervent than Tom could ever have expected.

"Tom, you . . . you got to find a reason for livin'. You just got to. You don't have no idea what endin' it that way does to ever'body, the people you leave behind."

"Ain't leavin' nobody behind, son."

Suddenly Jess's hand spun him around, and now there was as much anger in the younger man's face as there was compassion.

"You're leavin' *me*," snapped Jess. "Damn it, you're leavin' *me*."

Confused, Tom studied the blue-gray eyes, the lines at the dust-caked brow, the tight jaw with all its stubble. "You care that much?"

"Damned right I do. Damned right. I remember a eight-year-old boy watchin' his father shoot himself. I remember the awful years him growin' up without him. I remember him blamin' himself over and over for just standin' and watchin' instead of stoppin' him."

Tom's self-pity was suddenly forgotten in all the deep emotions he had stirred in Jess. "That how . . . how it was, son?"

The pain in Jess's face grew even more intense.

"Tom, ever'thing you do in this life's got a bearin' on ever'body that's around you. You got to

221

remember that. You just got to. I . . . I just don't know what else to say."

From the strain in Jess's voice, there was nothing more he could say. As the young man rose with glistening eyes and lowered head and wandered almost aimlessly toward the hackberries, Tom suddenly weighed his own need for closure against all that Jess had told him.

Overwhelmed by thoughts and emotions, Tom didn't think he would ever sleep again, but he must have dozed off as soon as he stretched out under the algerita bush. His dreams were ruled by vivid images of Sarah and a faceless seventeen-year-old girl whose fate seemed strangely entwined with hers across a gulf of twenty years. They both were calling his name and he couldn't answer, couldn't break the invisible bonds that held him speechless even as *"Tom . . . Tom"* continued to sound in his ears.

He opened his eyes to a sun setting through ribbons of orange in the pass's west notch. The currents still whispered his name. But as the moments passed, it dawned on him that it wasn't just *Tom* he heard, but something more.

"M-Mister T-Tom . . . M-Mister T-Tom."

When Tom looked, he saw the supine Dee almost imperceptibly lifting a hand in summons. Beyond, scattered out under the hackberries, the other 7L cowhands sprawled in obviously deep sleep.

It was easier for Tom to crawl the few feet to the boy than to try to rise. Dee was still mumbling his name when he reached his side.

"I'm here, young fellow," said Tom.

But now the teenager had fallen into oblivion again, although his index finger persisted in a slow, gesturing call. Tom took the hand in his callused palm, and when he squeezed it Dee opened his eyes. The boy seemed to spend long moments focusing, prompting Tom to reassure him.

"Young fellow," he said again, "I'm right here."

Those sunken eyes fixed on Tom's. "M-Mister T-Tom, am I fixin' to die, M-Mister T-Tom?"

Tom would rather have faced another Mexican butcher in a black blizzard than to answer. What could he tell him, the truth? That his condition was grim? That those terrible wounds were infected and that he was weak and feverish almost to the point of no return? Should he shoot straight and tell this poor, suffering orphan that the ordeals he had undergone could kill even now as surely as a .44 ball?

"T-Tell me, M-Mister T-Tom."

Tom placed a hand on his shoulder. "Ain't your time, young fellow."

"Th-Then how c-come my m-ma's been singin' to me? How come she's a-a-singin' right now, M-Mister T-Tom?"

Tom stared at him, seeing in those hollowed

eyes a reflection of things beyond this time and place. Maybe in those last moments Sarah's eyes had held similar mysteries, the same glimpses into a far-away world where there were no red devils or Mexican butchers or white-fanged wolves.

Tom just didn't know, and all he could do was concentrate on the needs of the here and now.

"I know you've a powerful thirst," he told the boy. "I'm fetchin' you some water."

Tom struggled to his feet and started for the arroyo, the dust rising from his shuffling boots.

"That you with M-Ma, M-Miss Sarah?"

Tom whirled.

"M-Miss Sarah," Dee went on. "H-How come you to d-die, M-Miss Sarah?"

Stunned, Tom stared at those trembling lips as he approached again.

"What is it you're a-sayin'?" asked Tom.

But now the lips were silent.

Kneeling, Tom gently shook Dee's shoulder. "Young fellow," he asked again, "what is it you're a-say—"

"Why-Why'd anybody wanna k-kill you that-away, M-Miss Sarah?"

Tom flinched, the memory of that .44 in his hand surging through him. Even though he was fully hydrated now, his mouth went as dry as the powdered alkali at Horsehead Crossing.

Dee's eyes closed again, and Tom extended

quivering fingers to the teenager's gaunt cheek, all too pale after days under a burning sun.

"You . . . You're a-seein' somethin'," Tom said. He swallowed hard. "Tell me what you're a-seein'."

All of a sudden Dee's eyes went wide and wild and distant, as if witnessing things nobody should know.

"Wh-What's that, M-Miss Sarah?" Dee whispered. "They gonna k-kill Liz Anne? Fixin' to k-kill her—them mud walls—same as you, M-Miss Sarah?"

Again the teenager drifted into unconsciousness—and then he began to shake.

"Young fellow, young fellow."

Tom gripped the boy's shoulders as though to hold back the shudder. Still, the convulsions persisted—thirty seconds, a minute, two minutes—before finally giving way to fitful sleep with breaths more labored than ever.

Tom wanted to ask more, much more, but this time the young cowhand responded neither to his voice nor his gentle touch. How could he rouse the poor kid again, break through to that other world to which the muzzle of a .44 had so unjustly banished Sarah?

Coming to his feet, Tom hurried away to the water holes. He was in the arroyo only a minute and then he rushed back, dripping a trail from his hat, but even as he put a hand on the boy's chest, he knew Dee was dead.

For the longest, Tom just sat at Dee's side, looking into the lifeless, staring eyes. He grieved for this innocent, backward kid in a way that he hadn't since Horsehead Crossing. Twice now, someone had died in his stead, and he couldn't understand why. He turned his face to the red-streaked dome above and just couldn't understand why.

But as he looked far across the heavens and deep within himself, he found one thing shining with the clarity of spring water—a mission.

His mission. The only one that could ever be for him, no matter what Jess had said. And it involved two women and Satan's brood at blood-stained adobe walls in a corner of hell called the Pecos.

Tom had never reclaimed his swollen-barreled .44, but he did so now, exchanging the .45 for it at Jess's side. Like the other 7L hands, Jess slept so soundly that he never stirred even as Tom reloaded and proceeded to unstake and saddle the roan. Leading it past Dee's forever stilled form, he dropped down into the shadowy arroyo and stopped at the water holes.

He gave the animal enough rein to water up, then sprawled to his stomach and slaked his thirst. When neither cowhand nor horse could drink any more, he struggled into the saddle and started through the gloom for the glow that showed low in the sky through Castle Gap's western cleft.

As the roan picked its way through the winding gorge, the hoofbeats echoing from the encroaching bluffs, Tom dwelled on Dee's words. His whole life, Tom had known only what his five senses had told him was true. He was at a loss to understand, much less accept, anything beyond what he could see and touch, smell and taste. And hear.

He had heard plenty secondhand from Dee, and the rational part of Tom told him that the feverish boy had merely incorporated Tom's account of the Horsehead fight into his dying delusion. That didn't explain Dee's use of the name Sarah, all right, but who was to say he hadn't been referring to some friend of his ma's? Was there any other name that graced so many family Bibles?

But in the dark of night, riding to his own grave, Tom listened only to what his emotions told him. Sarah had reached across time and space through a dying boy. She had cried out Tom's long-ago misdeed, and in so doing had ripped out what little remained of his heart.

But she had also done more. From on high, she had looked down on Liz Anne. She had seen the fate about to befall the girl, an end no less certain than her own. And both of them were calling him to those adobe walls to face alone so many things in life and death.

EIGHTEEN

Liz Anne could smell the Pecos for miles before she reached it.

The stench burned her sinuses and churned her stomach, and by the time her horse picked its way by moonlight down the final approach to Horsehead Crossing, she understood why. So many dead cows festered on the barren floodplain that she could have stepped from one maggot-infested rib cage to another for a solid mile. The treeless riverside that overlooked what seemed a sheer-walled moat was even more gruesome; in places the carcasses were piled four feet high, horrid monuments to the Big Dry of '86.

It was little wonder that men called this river the graveyard of the cowman's hopes—and now it had claimed the last vestiges of her hopes as well.

But where there was death, there was also life, in the form of bloodsucking mosquitoes that swarmed about Liz Anne's face. They tormented her relentlessly, but at least her hands were free of the saddle horn and she could fight them away. Perez had not let her travel without bonds out of any humanitarian consideration, but out of necessity. Ever since putting a little distance between themselves and Castle Gap, they had walked and only occasionally switched to their jaded horses, all the while keeping an eye out behind for rising dust that would signal pursuit.

Perez pulled rein along the sudden bank and the other horses stopped with him. Ten feet below, Liz Anne could see the distorted glow of the moon in the rolling river, a cauldron as swift as a race horse but ominous in its silence. Every so often, a floating mass caught moonlight in its sweep downstream, the fleeting presence adding to the Styx-like feel of this place.

"There," said Perez, motioning upstream.

In the direction he pointed, the high, vertical bank seemed to give way to a brief stretch that fell gently toward the dark waters. With Perez in the lead, the party trailed upriver, maneuvering between carcasses, and found more dead cattle as they dropped down the miry slope. At stream's edge, they held their mounts and studied the crossing.

Liz Anne liked what she saw—treacherous currents that surely could end her suffering before her horse might gain the cut bank fifty feet across and a little downstream.

But now the three Mexicans were all speaking at once, their voices rising as they gestured to the river. Liz Anne didn't need to be fluent in Spanish to recognize that they argued, and the smattering of words she did understand told her plenty. Perez wanted to cross now, establishing the river as a buffer against their pursuers so they could rest and seek forage before pushing on for Chihuahua. But the other men contended that a night crossing was too dangerous and wanted to wait until daylight.

Finally, the brunt of Perez's will won out, and one after the other, his confederates forced their mounts into the river as he and Liz Anne looked on.

The hoofs must have bogged as the horses entered the water, for the animals seemed to have difficulty extricating their legs. The riders managed only a few feet before the depth demanded that their horses swim, and from there to the far bank men and animals splashed and struggled as the current threatened to carry them away. As it was, the waters swept the horses several yards downstream before they reached solid footing again at the opposite cut.

At Perez's gesture and a few coarse words in Spanish, Liz Anne urged her mount into the crossing. As soon as the waters rose about her legs, she gave the animal its head and withdrew her boots from the stirrups. She could feel the current's power as it surged right-to-left against her thigh and swept over the horse's withers.

Suddenly her mount was squealing, lunging, swimming, entirely submerged below the neck. Only her fragile grip on the bridle kept her from being borne away. In another few moments she was in mid-stream, the boiling waters all but consuming her. Through her mind flashed memories of Jess and the unspeakable act that Perez had perpetrated against her—polar images in conflict with one another.

One was a dream of what might have been, the other a nightmare reality that could never be undone.

With a quick prayer, Liz Anne released her hold.

She sank, the dark waters swirling about her, singeing her nostrils, muffling the sound of her instinctive struggles. She popped up, the reek of the stream unbearable in her face as a witch's brew laced with hair and maggots burned her mouth and throat. Then something seized her from behind and wouldn't let go, and she turned to see Perez in the moonlight, one hand clinging to his horse's bridle and his shriveled appendage clutching her collar.

Liz Anne fought as she had never fought before. She struck at his elbow, shoulder, face, and when that failed, she tried dragging him down with her. She had no leverage, but the current's relentless force from upstream and the pull of two riders from downriver were just too much for the exhausted horse. Rolling to its side, it shed Perez's hand and cast the two of them into the frothy currents.

An undertow sucked Liz Anne into the depths, but she resurfaced just as quickly, Perez's fingers still gripping her collar. Caught in a raging tide that wouldn't be denied, they bobbed on downstream in a frightful dance, Perez's terrible grimace a moonlit mask in her face every time Liz Anne came up.

He cursed her and shouted for his confederates, but mere words couldn't cope with the river's fury. As the waters rose and fell, spinning Liz Anne at their mercy, she was vaguely aware of the receding ford, where Perez's horse approached the far bank while the second animal turned back.

From upstream a black mass suddenly came surging at eye level, the tossing carcass of a cow bloated almost beyond recognition. It struck Liz Anne and Perez broadside, a crushing blow by bone and sinew that separated the two as it drove her under water.

She surfaced, too far from Perez for him to clutch her again. Now there remained only for her to end her life, but as she ceased her struggles she found that death by intentional drowning was not an easy thing. The more she relaxed, the more buoyant she became, and try as she might every time she went under, she just couldn't bring herself to inhale water into her lungs.

Perez disappeared in the violent currents, but his cries must have had some effect, for against the sky's muted light, Liz Anne caught the silhouettes of riders keeping pace high on the west-side bank. They trailed alongside as the river broke sharply to the left, then back to the right. At another snaking bend to the left, Liz Anne saw a dark, motionless pile suddenly looming across her course. It rose a full yard above her head, a dam of sorts jutting from the west wall's base and impeding the flow for half the river's width.

The next instant she was upon it, the victim in a wrenching collision that lifted her out of the water and deposited her across a spongy mass more pungent than even the waters. She lay there panting and desperate, her legs tossing in the swirling currents. Something glassy alongside her cheek reflected moonlight, and the moment she recognized it for what it was, she cried out and recoiled involuntarily.

There were two of them actually, dead eyes staring out of a cow's misshapen and rotting head. Liz Anne didn't know what hell was like, but she figured this must be it, a river dammed by bloated carcasses that crawled with maggots.

Just as she clambered to her knees, something slapped her ear and settled around her back and upper arms. The coil snapped taut, wrenching the breath from her, and abruptly she was in the grip of an unyielding force dragging her toward the overhead bank. She tried to cry out but she had no air, and as the rope cut into her skin she slammed into a hewn wall of packed alkali. All the way to the sky that twisted overhead, she felt the bank's abrasive slide against her torso.

Liz Anne knew what was happening, and there was nothing she could do but surrender to the inevitable and lament her inability to drown herself. By the loop of a catch-rope and the power of a horse, the swine who did Perez's bidding had thwarted her last chance to die with dignity.

Perez was drowning, and there was no one to help him.

He thrashed wildly, the black waters swamping and spitting him out in terrible cycle. He gulped great amounts of putrid brine and clawed at a sheer bank that teased and denied as it surged past. He was caught in a hell of his own making, and as the merciless current swept him closer to judgment, he strangely thought of the elderly gringo who had abused him for so long.

Perez was just a boy, cast aside by a whore of a mother, but the old man had him by the scruff of the neck. They were before a water trough, and the viejo was drowning him by wicked degrees. For the third time the vise-like hand plunged the boy's face under water, holding it there while Perez fought futilely in a tempest of swirling bubbles. Each time that the gringo dragged him up choking and gasping, Perez was a little closer to death, until finally the waters went dark and so did his world.

Perez had eventually awakened, all right, but his subsequent life at the hands of the dominating old man had been worse than any death he could have imagined.

Until now.

This was a cesspool of a river, so ridden with carrion that it would have been a blight even in perdition. He could smell it and taste it and feel the bump of the carcasses as they floated by. If this place was an omen of the punishment to come, Perez had to forestall the end as long as possible.

He didn't know how many bends he navigated, how many times the current threw him into dirt banks that sprang a dozen vertical feet to the moonlit sky. But now his strength was waning. The moon and walls and rushing tide's undulations came only in flashes, interspersed by ever-increasing periods of black whorls where air didn't exist.

Perez was underwater with hopes all but gone when the current drove him hard into something as unbudging as it was bony. Suddenly he was wrapped around it, head to foot, the pressure of the surging waters a potent force against his back. But a powerful undertow was at work as well, trying to suck his leg below the obstruction and pull the rest of him along with it.

Perez groped desperately, finding a hold above his head and another beyond that. It took all his remaining strength, but he succeeded in dragging himself up to air just as he thought his lungs would burst.

He was belly-down across cattle carcasses that extended from a silt deposit against the left bank. A few rushes grew here, and the mosquitoes were already buzzing around Perez's ears. But what seized his attention was the sloughing ledge that angled all the way up to the bank's summit.

Perez didn't know if it was a freak of erosion or a trail beaten by animals seeking water. All he cared was that it was a way out of hell. He scrambled across to the rushes, fought the quicksand's powerful suction against his boots, and climbed to the top.

He stood weak-kneed in the bathing moonlight and tried to get his bearings. He was disoriented after all the crooks of the river, and the moon had reversed positions, now hanging beyond the channel where it shouldn't have been. Confused, Perez replayed the desperate moments in the stream. Just which bank had he scaled?

He considered the right-to-left flow at Horsehead Crossing and the frantic sweep downstream, then checked the moon's sparkle in the rolling currents below. He was on the Castle Gap side of the Pecos, but east and west were all mixed up.

Perez shouted across the river for Rodriguez and Ernesto, but with all the sharp bends they could just as easily have been in the opposite direction. Lost in the coils, he called out left and right as he trudged upstream, knowing that he had to hug the bank if he were to find the crossing.

As he traced the river's snake-track, the moon seemed caught in a frenzied dance. In one brief span, the orb completely circled him in the sky. With his legs quivering and the wound in his cheek throbbing, Perez grew increasingly frustrated, even alarmed, at his inability to escape this maze, and he directed all manner of curses against his confederates. He shouted repeatedly that he was their capitan and that their throats would taste the steel of his blade unless they crossed to this side of the river again and rescued him. Still, the only answer was the incessant whine of mosquitoes about his face until a saddle rattled from behind.

He heard the cock of a revolver as he whirled to a shadowy rider forty paces away through the creosote and mounds of dead cattle.

"Quien es—who is it!" demanded Perez, whipping out his six-shooter.

He didn't wait for an answer, not when sights may have been upon him. He fired from the hip for the horse's breast, only to feel the metallic click of hammer against unresponsive cartridge.

Madre de Dios! His powder was wet!

"Quien es! Rodriguez? Ernesto?"

He answered his own question with another half-dozen empty snaps of firing pin against dead cartridges.

The dark rider began to move against the moonlit sky, the horse's silhouette growing in size. Perez began to flee, his water-logged boots stumbling in the alkali. Hoofs pounded the turf behind him, and he looked back over his shoulder at a charging horse about to run him over.

The Mexican's only chance was to throw himself into the river, but that would have been worse than no chance at all. At the last instant he tried to dodge the barreling shadow, but the animal veered with him as deftly as a cutting horse after a calf. The next thing Perez knew, striding legs were upon him, and he went down in a dark blur of hoofs and horse flesh against a wildly spinning sky.

He must have taken a hard blow to the head, for when he regained his senses he was lying in the dirt with his hands tied at his back. Another bond was around his neck, and when it abruptly tightened and threatened to strangle, he looked around and followed the lariat's course up to a rider. The moon was just right to illuminate his face—the crusted skin cancers, the deep scoring at the temples, the gray stubble that told his age. But of all his features, the eyes that squinted even in the moonlight struck Perez the most. They were like those of the old gringo who had raised him, eyes that stared and judged and dominated.

"Capitan, hell," the stranger rasped with sarcasm. "Just a screwworm blowin' at a good person's ever' little scratch. Get up."

When Perez didn't move immediately, the rider dallied the rope around the horn and backed his horse a little, choking Perez as he dragged him through the dirt. Even when the lariat relaxed, the Mexican continued to wheeze as he writhed under the moon.

"Said, 'Get up!'" the rider repeated.

His neck burning from the fibers, Perez now did his best to do so, but without the use of his hands he simply couldn't comply. Finally the rider came closer, reeling-in the lariat until he literally dragged him up by the neck.

The old man motioned upriver. "Start walkin', you son of a bitch. All the way to hell!"

Coughing and gasping for air, the Mexican began to stumble forward like a dog on a leash. Perez may have been more dead than not, but the rider nevertheless had awakened something in him. It was hatred, obsessive hatred, not just for the abusive viejo of his youth but for every aging gringo in all the years since.

And nothing could satisfy it except to kill the man at the other end of the rope.

NINETEEN

Upriver, Tom picked up a loose horse, but he and the Mexican continued on as they had, with Tom in the stirrups and leading the saddled stray, and the prisoner afoot with a noose around his neck.

A great fire burned inside Tom, urging him to gig his animal and drag the SOB to death. More than once he was on the verge of touching spurs to the roan, but if the vermin at rope's end was indeed capitan of those whoresons across the river, he would hold his vengeance in check for a while. Still, as he remembered the two good men—one of them a boy, really—who had died because of these sons of hell, and the girl who must have endured something far worse, he took grim pleasure in yanking the rope and hearing the Mexican gurgle.

They traced the dramatic bends all the way to river's edge at Horsehead Crossing, a site indelibly burned in Tom's memory. A lot of blood stained these banks, but he didn't dwell on the untold wagoners or stage passengers or cattle drovers who had bled out their share. He thought only of the fifteen emigrants who had come here in search of tomorrow, only to find a place not in life but in death.

The guilt crushed Tom yet again, guilt for surviving, for perpetrating what he had at those mud walls just upriver. At least in a little while, just as soon as he completed his mission, he could finally make amends to Sarah and all those other good people.

He brought the second horse up alongside on his left and snubbed it by the reins to the saddle horn.

"Get on him," Tom ordered.

The Mexican turned to the horse, then back to Tom.

"Keep a-standin' there, you SOB," added Tom, "and I swear to God I'll drag you clean across them flats."

The Mexican obediently moved, Tom allowing him enough rope to reach the bay's on-side. When he was across the horse from Tom, the Mexican paused, but seemed afraid to test him with a glance up. Tom understood his hesitation; with hands tied behind his back, he couldn't climb on.

Tom reeled-in the rope until the noose was firm against the bandido's windpipe. "Get your boot in the stirrup or I'll hang you right here."

"*Maria purisima!*" the Mexican whispered. "How hell can—"

Tom tightened the rope, cutting off the Mexican's air. Even in the moonlight, Tom could see the panic on the swarthy face. Those dark eyes bulged and the veins at his temples swelled, but Tom knew that the Mexican was now doing all he could to comply. With the noose providing balance at terrible price, the *bandido* finally found the stirrup and tried to step on. Still, he was half-dead before Tom dragged him up across the bay.

Tom kept the horse snubbed as he lifted his revolver skyward and squeezed off a shot that startled both animals. While the blast still echoed, he released the bay and quickly maneuvered the roan so that the wheezing Mexican shielded him from the far bank.

"Hombres!" Tom called across the river. "Your capitan for that girl you got!" He jerked the rope at the Mexican's neck, gaining his attention. "Speak Meskin to 'em!"

Tom could tell by his prisoner's face just how unexpected all this was, but the Mexican wasted no time in seizing the opportunity. Turning to the opposite cut, he found enough air to shout a pair of names repeatedly and rattle off a quick salvo of Spanish that Tom recognized as a rough translation.

For a minute that seemed an hour, there were only the buzz of mosquitoes and quiet snort of Tom's horse as if it had rollers in its nose. Then a disembodied voice called from across the river.

"Perez!"

"The señorita!" the Mexican shouted back. "Get her!"

"Have 'em let her swim her horse across," Tom ordered. "Soon as she's in the water, I'll start you across from this side." Tom tugged the rope a little. "This thing stays around your neck, tied hard and fast to my saddle. If they go and shoot me—if I ain't here to cut it when it all feeds out —your horse'll keep on swimmin' but you'll be back a-drownin'."

242

Tom's words must have been clear, for he could see the Mexican pale in the moonlight even as the bandido relayed the message.

"The señorita!" the prisoner reiterated when he finished. "Do it, cabrons! Do it!"

The Mexican continued to demand that they comply, but the far bank went silent and Tom figured that the disembodied voice had withdrawn. He didn't know what to anticipate, and as the minutes passed he began to worry that the girl might mean more to them than their capitan. But finally there appeared in the far cut's gloom a trio of riders too shadowy to identify.

"They a girl with 'em?" pressed Tom. "Have her say somethin'."

"Hellcat not talk much," contended the Mexican.

Tom took the initiative. "Girl?" he called out. "Miss Liz Anne, you over there?"

Only a troubling silence reigned, and Tom tightened the noose around the Mexican's throat. "She there or not?" he demanded. "She—"

"Who is it?" called a feminine voice. "Who's there?"

"Name's Tom! I come to get you!"

Again, that ominous quiet ruled the night for the longest.

"Young lady!" Tom shouted again. "I'm here to take you back!"

"Just kill me, let me die!"

A terrible rage swept over Tom, and he pulled

the rope so strongly that he could feel it sink into the Mexican's neck.

"What is it you done to her!" he growled. "What the hell you done?"

As the Mexican began to gasp and gurgle again, Tom lifted his gaze back to the riders. "Start her across, or so help me God I'll kill him right now!"

Tom supposed that they didn't need a translation, for one of the bandidos led the girl's horse down to the water. The capitan was still struggling for breath, but Tom used his own pony's bulk to force the Mexican's mount to the stream's brink, while at the same time continuing to use him as a shield.

"*Manos*," gasped the Mexican, looking back at Tom and wiggling his bound hands against his back in reminder.

Tom only smiled grimly.

"Por favor! Cut me loose!" pleaded the Mexican. "Rio bad! Muy bad!"

"Better keep them feet in the stirrups. Me, I'll be a-keepin' this noose around your neck, let it play out little at a time. Don't think for a minute I won't sure as hell drown you if it comes to it."

The Mexican continued to protest, but as soon as the girl's horse entered the water, Tom slapped the bay on the rump.

"Gig him," Tom ordered with a wave of his revolver. "Gig him or I'll shoot you dead right here!"

The Mexican's face was a mask of fear as he urged the horse into the river. As the animal met underlying quicksand in the shallows and began to lunge, the rider had trouble staying astride, and the situation grew only worse when the bay struck swimming water. The currents began to whip the rope that trailed out behind the Mexican, but Tom had a half-wrap around the saddle horn and controlled every sliding inch.

The girl's horse began to struggle, and Tom momentarily had second thoughts about forcing this exchange by moonlight. But noon or midnight made no difference to a horse with night vision, and her animal held its own even as only its head and neck showed. Tom had risked much on a young girl's horsemanship, but she evidently knew enough to slip her feet out of the stirrups and seize the bridle.

At mid-stream the two horses bumped, and for an awful moment Tom feared the worst, then the girl's pony brushed past and the Mexican was beyond her, his head bobbing as he tried to keep from being swept away. Again and again he cried out, only to have his words muffled by swamping waters.

Tom knew that as soon as he freed the Mexican's noose, those firearms beyond the river would light up the night. He tightened his grip, slowing the rope's advance, trying to buy the girl more time to get across. Still, with a 35-foot rope in a 50-foot river, his only viable option was to do something dramatic.

Just as the capitan reached lariat's end, Tom backed his roan, the sudden force yanking the Mexican off the bay. An instant later, Tom whipped out his knife and severed the rope, casting the Mexican adrift.

As the riders across-river splashed their horses into the crossing in attempted rescue, the girl's pony found the quicksand-laden shallows before Tom. He met her in the water and lunged for the bridle, gripping the cheek long enough for her to find stirrups and reins.

As her horse began to carry her up the slope, Tom lifted his revolver against the Pecos and saw a dark whirlpool of men and animals in the surging waters. One horse and rider had turned back for the bank, and Tom fired a quick shot that missed before wheeling the roan and chasing after the girl.

They were in an exposed position under the moon's flooding light as he quickly overtook her, the alkali flying from the hoofs. Any moment that bandido would summit the far bank and have them squarely in his sights, and there was no place in hell to take cover on this barren plain.

Except . . .

"This a-way!" he yelled, cutting his horse upstream.

The girl veered with him, then a rifle cracked

and her squealing horse went down, rolling her across the flat.

"Young lady!" exclaimed Tom, pulling rein.

She was moaning and shaking her head, but her mount was as dead as the rotting carcasses that looked on in mute witness. By force of spurs, Tom circled back as another slug whizzed by in ricochet.

"Young lady! Young lady!" he cried, reaching down with a hand as he came abreast.

She seemed a little dazed, but she lifted an arm and Tom clutched it. More gunfire rocked the night, the bullets thudding into a nearby carcass, but finally he managed to drag her up behind the cantle and resumed their desperate flight upriver.

The jaded horse struggled under the double burden, but Tom kept it in a gallop around a ninety-degree bend to the left, dodging dead cattle all the way. The hoofs fell into old wagon ruts along the bank, and when another slug sliced through Tom's hat brim, he checked the opposing bluff and saw a shadowy horseman keeping pace.

Sarah! They's on us, Sarah! Them red devils is on us!

In another three hundred yards, the Pecos twisted even more sharply to the left, almost turning back on itself, and just as the roan negotiated the bend another boom of the rifle set the horse stumbling. For a moment Tom thought the animal would regain its stride, but there was blood at its shoulder as more shots reverberated. Suddenly the saddle dropped out from under him and there was no place to go but over the horse's head.

Tom hadn't taken a fall like this in years. He tumbled and ate dirt and watched moon and sky whirl crazily, and when it was over he was sprawled in the alkali and more lead was pitting the ground about him. He found the girl close by, then rolled to her so that a carcass was between them and the shooter.

"You all right, girl?"

She didn't answer but she was stirring, and Tom glanced back at the dead horse and knew he had to retrieve his powder flask and bullet bag. But not only did the items look to be pinned under the animal, a drumming of hoofs now rose up from downriver. In moments he and the girl would be caught in a crossfire, and the carcasses would shield them from one shooter only to expose them to another.

Through the twisted horn of a festering steer in his face, Tom scanned the sprawling flat inside the bend. Eighty yards away, past carcasses and creosote and bare alkali, dark ruins rose up, ghostly in the moonlight.

A chance, Sarah! The only chance we got!

"See them walls?" Tom demanded of the girl. "Soon's I go to shootin', start a-runnin'!"

He didn't wait for her to acknowledge, for those

pounding hoofs were almost upon them. He seized the steer horn and fired across the river as he pulled himself up, then stumbled after Sarah-who-wasn't-Sarah for the very walls that had haunted him for twenty years.

Gunfire erupted from behind, but all he and the girl could do was duck and dodge and keep staggering on. Already he had expended three shots, and he couldn't afford to fire a fourth in mere deterrence.

The ruins seemed just as distant as they had on that other dark day when he and Sarah had fought their way toward it. His legs seemed just as slow, the strafing bullets just as fast. The alkali seemed every bit as grasping, the pursuit equally swift. Then abruptly the two of them were there, clambering over the crumbling adobe, falling inside melting walls as uneven in height as a graveyard fence with broken pickets.

Finally Tom had come back, for the first time since his rescuers, fearing another Comanche attack, had hastily scooped out a shallow excavation beside Sarah's body. They had shoveled dirt into her face and quickly wagoned him away, but he now seemed closer to her than in all the years of aim-less wandering. Maybe it was because at this very moment he lay across her unmarked grave.

Jess was back at that awful shed again, in dream, only this time he was fully grown and the man through the crack was not his father, but Tom.

Yet every other detail was the same: the distraught face with beads of sweat, the cap-and-ball revolver at the graying temple, the trembling finger sliding inside the trigger guard. Jess could even smell the fresh pine planks again and feel the bleeding sap sticky around his eye socket, and yet he seemed to know that this was another time and place—and more.

It was a second chance to burst inside that door and change so many things that had haunted him all these years.

"Jess . . . Jess."

Why was Gabe suddenly there too, shaking his shoulder and whispering his name? What connection could he possibly have with this demon that Jess had to rid himself of once and for all?

"Jess. Jess, you better come here. It's Dee."

Jess opened his eyes to see Gabe's silhouette kneeling over him. By the position of the moon past his shoulder, daybreak was only hours away, but Jess suddenly feared that the night was only beginning.

"It's Dee, Jess," repeated a shaken Gabe. "I think he's dead."

Jess sat bolt upright, his heart racing.

"And Tom's took a horse and lit out," Gabe added.

Jess stayed silent as he came to his feet and turned toward Dee's dark outline across the small clearing. The boy had been like a ward to him, a backward kid with nobody in the world except the 7L bunch. It had been a responsibility that Dee had never asked him to assume, but Jess had gladly borne it.

And now Dee was gone because Jess hadn't had the heart to make him stay behind, no matter how much the orphan had worshipped Liz Anne.

"Dead, is he?" spoke up a drowsy voice from behind. "Tried tellin' you you's a damned fool for bringin' him. That worthless kid wasn't—"

Even as Jess turned, Gabe was already bolting for Sorrels, who stirred on the ground under an adjacent hackberry. Sorrels had just raised himself to an elbow, his lips still spewing disrespect, when Gabe's boot swept out of the gloom and struck him viciously in the face.

"No more!" cried Gabe as Sorrels fell back. "You ain't sayin' no more!"

But maybe Sorrels had a right to cast blame, thought Jess. Maybe he had been right about everything. Dee was dead, and the fault rested squarely on Jess's shoulders and nobody else's.

He started for Dee's body, the burden crushing him more with every step. Dee was dead. He was gone and nothing could ever bring him back— not regret or guilt or Gabe's boot against Sorrels's jaw.

He stopped over the still form and stared down at the colorless face, the mangled neck, the bloody bandages unraveling. The lifeless eyes held moonlight, but they also reflected a dark and sudden hole in Jess's soul. The boy had looked up to him and trusted his judgment, and in payment Jess had let the wolves maul him and the sun finish off what was left.

"He's wrong, Jess."

Jess was aware that Gabe had come up beside him, but he maintained his painful stare at Dee.

"You hear me, Jess? Sorrels—he's wrong what he said."

Still, Jess didn't turn. "I . . . I thought you'd be sayin' it too, Gabe. You hadn't been shy about holdin' back about much of anything lately."

Gabe went silent for long seconds, and when he spoke again, emotion shaded his words. "I guess I'm just a ol' scared-y cat of the worst kind. But with water and vittles in me, I can sure see things a whole lot clearer now."

Jess felt a hand on his upper arm, and he faced his longtime friend to listen to his cracking voice.

"I know what Dee meant to you, partner," Gabe went on. "I-I know what that little booger meant to the both of us."

Jess wanted to say something, but the words would only hang in his throat.

"What you figure about Tom?" Gabe asked.

Jess looked back down at the boy's eyes, still shining blankly in the night. "He must've knowed about Dee. He's at Horsehead Crossin', and he's not there just to get Liz Anne back. I won't be neither. We get Dee buried, we can be there ourselves come daybreak."

An hour later, the three of them were ready to ride, but Jess took a moment to stand face-to-face with a thoroughly subdued Sorrels, whose broken nose still bled.

"We're goin' into a den of snakes," Jess told him. "Like it or not, I'll be carryin' your Winchester." He shoved Dee's .45 into Sorrels's hand. "I'm countin' on you usin' this thing right."

TWENTY

Three balls in the cylinder, three butchers in the night.

Tom had no margin for error.

But how long could he risk just waiting, feeling the heat radiate from the intersecting mud walls at his breast and shoulder? He and the girl were taking fire from multiple directions, three distinct firearms piercing the stillness as the slugs chipped away at the fragile bricks of alkali and straw. When would those bandidos figure out he was low on powder and launch an all-out assault?

He had to deter them with return gunfire, and yet he couldn't. Still, if they all breached these walls at once, would he have a chance in hell of taking them out one ball to the man? When he would see them as only a whirlwind of dark shadows?

"How come you to do this? How come, mister?"

Liz Anne was beside him, huddled at wall's base, but Tom continued to concentrate on the shrapnel that flew from the adobe with every *crack!* of that big rifle.

"Mister?"

"Ever'body deserves a chance, young lady," said Tom. "They tried takin' yours away."

Suddenly her fingers sank into his arm, and he turned to see the moonlight delineating a face so hopeless, the glistening eyes showing only as dark windows into a broken soul.

"Just let me die—all I want's to die!"

There was rage inside Tom, against those sons of bitches who had violated her, but there was also such humanity that the words he wanted to say died in his choking throat at first.

"Ain't your fault," he finally managed. "Ain't none of it your fault. You gotta find a reason for livin'—and you got one, a good one."

Liz Anne just stared at him, stared and wept and shook uncontrollably.

"They's a good man back there wants to marry you," Tom went on. "He's chased after you all this way, through storms and desert and rock slides and ever'thing else."

Those eyes continued to stare, but now they

seemed to hold so much confusion, so many questions.

"I reckon," added Tom, "you know who I'm a-talkin' about."

"Jess?" she asked tentatively. "Jess is back there?"

"At the gap, just a few hours ago."

She whirled away, burying her face in her hands. "No! He mustn't know! He mustn't ever know!"

Tom placed a compassionate hand on her shoulder. "Them's bad hombres out there. They might've took a lot of things from you, but don't let 'em take away tomorrow too."

Tom wondered if either of them would see a tomorrow. At least in his case, he would die where he had intended, inside these forsaken ruins that had drawn him across all the terrible years. He would fall right here, just as Sarah had fallen, and he would bleed out across her grave in atonement for what he had done.

But Liz Anne—she had her whole life ahead of her, just as Sarah had once had, and he swore to do his best to bring this girl so cherished by Jess another sunrise, and many more after that.

The trouble was, Tom just didn't think his best would be good enough.

The hours wore on, and as Tom listened to the night, he suddenly didn't like what he heard.

Nothing.

No crack of a rifle or blast of a revolver. No

furious rain of exploding mud or *zing!* of a sailing ricochet. Not even the quiet rasp of a bullet as it slid into a cylinder, or cock of a spring-loaded hammer.

The silence was more ominous than anything Tom had experienced. Then an adobe brick tumbled from behind, and he spun with the .44 to look past a stairstepping inner partition. At the far end of the ruins, a little deeper in the river's coil, a hand gripped the top of the low outside wall.

There was a dark shape rising above it and Tom fired, the powder charge flashing against nearby patterned brick. The silhouette fell away and Tom frantically swept the gun barrel across the perimeter, looking for another attempted breach.

He caught a wisp of movement along the riverfront side, then Liz Anne shouted a warning and he wheeled again, one hundred eighty degrees to the recessed corner two arm-lengths away. Over melted brick to its left loomed a muzzle, and behind it was a face he recognized as the capitan's.

Tom fired without aiming, shattering adobe and throwing a blinding spray into the Mexican's eyes. The capitan disappeared, but Tom didn't have time to trace his course. He pivoted back to the wisp, but now it was gone.

Once more, only that dreadful quiet ruled the Pecos except for the ringing in Tom's ears.

Coming about yet again, Tom scrambled up and

peered over the fractured wall, hoping against hope to find the capitan's body and a firearm loaded for defense. But there was nothing except desert shadows painted by ruins and creosote and dead cattle.

He kept a low profile as he reassured the girl with a touch, then rushed on bum leg across meltdown and layered brick to the point where he had seen the hand. This time he did more than hope—he prayed with all the passion of Dee—but the ground beyond stretched barren except for those putrefying carcasses.

Tom had repelled the attack, all right, but at terrible cost.

One ball in the cylinder, three butchers in the night.

He crept back to the girl and huddled beside her in silence. The moon was low in the sky now, but a ray fell through the ruins and played in the streamlined curves of his Army Colt. He turned it sideways and stared at the walnut stock and brass trigger guard, the sprinkle of rust in the metal backstrap and the powder residue along the frame. He didn't need to check the cylinders for the single load that remained, but he did so anyway, because there was nothing else he could do.

When those whoresons killed him, they'd cross the Pecos and strike out for Mexico with Liz Anne. Jess would have nobody left to depend on, but he'd track them down anyway, one against three, and Tom had already proven that those odds just wouldn't work. In the end, there would be another good man dead in all of this, and Liz Anne would still be as violated.

Tom was out of options, except for one too horrible to contemplate, but as he turned the barrel upright and leaned his forehead against it, he dwelled on it nevertheless. He could feel the hot steel, smell the fouled gunpowder, see a streak of moonlight in the contours of the notched cylinder.

"You aren't reloadin'," said Liz Anne.

Tom wouldn't look at her.

"They're comin' back, and you're not reloadin'," she went on.

Tom closed his eyes, remembering.

With a choking sob of realization, Liz Anne seized his arm, the fingers digging into his skin.

"Just one—if you saved one—don't let them take me!" she pleaded.

Tom swallowed hard. "You got no idea what you're askin' of me," he rasped.

"Promise me! You've got to promise me!"

He held his silence even against her wrenching sobs, but when she buried her face against Sarah's grave and her shoulders began to shake, it was like a dagger through Tom's heart.

About the time that dawn began to break, the long-range gunfire resumed. The adobe disintegrated and the ricochets flew, and the only thing Tom could do was sit there with head

258

hanging against revolver barrel and ponder that awful option. Once before, he had weighed such a decision, and he had chosen wrongly.

Yet, then as now, the alternative had seemed unspeakable.

He glanced at the girl who still sobbed across Sarah's grave. No matter his choice, she deserved so much better. Jess deserved so much better, and yet only Tom could decide.

Suddenly he heard a growing thunder, and he sprang up to peer over the crumbling wall into a burnt orange sky. He saw three riders abreast, charging out of the dawn, the dust billowing as the frenzied hoofs churned the alkali. The silhouettes were firing as they came, the slugs shattering adobe at Tom's left, his right, the partition behind.

The sons of perdition had finally had enough, and they were determined to end it here and now.

Tom dropped and swung to Liz Anne. She looked up at him, and for a moment he just stared at her, convicted by the desperate plea in that pitiful haunted face.

"Close your eyes," said Tom. "Just look away and close your eyes."

Tom thought he could read the start of a silent prayer on her lips as she turned her head. She laid it peacefully across Sarah's last resting place, as if the alkali was a comforting pillow, and Tom hoped that Sarah would be waiting for her on the other side to embrace and welcome and love.

Tom turned the eight-inch barrel toward her and eased the muzzle down behind her ear until strands of wind-blown hair played against the sight. The weapon had never seemed this heavy, a terrible burden quaking in his hand, but he slipped his finger inside the tarnished trigger guard and thumbed back the hammer almost tenderly. With a click that could be heard across twenty years, the cylinder revolved and locked into place, one last load ready to kill.

Tom closed his eyes, begging for forgiveness, the pad of his fingertip gently brushing the trigger's smooth curvature.

Suddenly it was as if it was Sarah at the end of that barrel, Sarah who he was defending against sons of hell storming out of a dawn rent by gunfire. He had to squeeze that trigger, keep those red devils from violating her again and again, but his arm was about her shoulders and he could feel something wet and sticky against his wrist. Opening his eyes, he saw Sarah's head hanging limply to the side, blood running from the corner of her mouth.

Sarah!

Sarah!

He cried out but she couldn't hear, couldn't feel the .44 muzzle beside her ear. He lowered the weapon without ever squeezing the trigger and took her face between his hands, turning it so that he could look into her eyes.

260

Sarah!

Sarah!

But she would never hear again, because those blue eyes were dilated and blank and staring into forever, and there was an oozing red hole in her breast.

With a start, Tom awoke to 1886 and knew what he had not known across all these years of regret and guilt. At the same instant, he heard a Winchester boom, then a shotgun and a .45, and he whirled to the mud wall and jumped up to look over.

The breast of a barreling horse was almost upon him, in its wake a revolver muzzle and the scowl of a capitan possessed. Beyond, Tom could see Jess and the 7L riders bursting out of the breaking sunrise, their second volley knocking the other bandidos from their mounts.

Tom fired his last load point-blank, a split second ahead of the capitan. The Mexican's shot went wide, but Tom's ball dropped the pony to its knees and momentum did the rest. Eight hundred pounds of dead horse plowed into the wall, collapsing a section and throwing the bandido forward.

Tom was vaguely aware that Liz Anne scrambled away, but the only thing he could do was catch the butcher as he flew at him over the animal's head. They fell back across Sarah's grave, a young man and an old one wallowing in the dirt and fighting over the Mexican's weapon.

261

The capitan reeked with the river's filth, but his vengeful eyes were even filthier, burning with a degree of depravity that Tom had never seen even in those Comanches.

The six-shooter flashed one way and then another in the sunlight, and suddenly Tom lost his tenuous hold. But he was still at such close quarters that it was the cylinder, not the muzzle, that gnawed at his ribs.

With the foulest of oaths, the Mexican pulled free and went bolt-upright on his knees so that he was framed against a sky streaked red. The glinting barrel swung around, and Tom was helpless across Sarah's grave as a thumb yanked back the hammer.

A blast rocked the ruins, and Tom wondered why he didn't feel more pain. But now the capitan's arms had gone limp, the eyes rolling up into their sockets, and the next instant the Mexican fell face-first in the Pecos alkali.

"Liz Anne! Liz Anne!"

Tom turned at the cry and pushed himself up, perching on his hip. Past the dead horse, he saw the nose of a bay with Jess above, the butt of a Winchester still against his shoulder. Tom exchanged glances with the girl, curled so heart-breakingly in a fetal position under an intact wall that hid her from Jess.

"Tom!" Jess exclaimed. "Liz Anne! Where's Liz Anne!"

There was still fear, even self-loathing, in the girl's face when Tom looked at her again, but he also found longing, the beginning of hope.

"It's all right," Tom told her. "You know you want to. It's all right."

There was a moment of indecision in her eyes, but when Jess called her name once more she burst to her feet, scrambled over the wall, ran for him.

Tom had never seen such happiness in anyone's face as that which swept over Jess.

"My Lord!" the young man cried. "Liz Anne! Oh my Lord! My Lord!"

Jess dropped from the horse just in time to accept the girl into his arms, and the two of them just stood there against the bright sunrise hugging and sobbing and saying each other's names again and again.

But Tom had his own revelation to digest, and he took up his .44 from the grave and hung his head against the upright barrel, just as he had done throughout so many dark and lonely days. He had always seemed closer to Sarah this way, and he needed this one last moment with her, so they could dwell together on all the things for which he had wrongly damned himself for twenty years. He knew now that she and the Good Lord were smiling at him from somewhere, and that when the time came, Sarah's arms would be just as wide to receive and embrace as Jess's had been for Liz Anne.

"Tom? What are you doin', Tom?"

Tom looked around and found a suddenly ashen Jess starting toward him. Still, Tom kept his forehead against the barrel as he clung to that special moment with Sarah.

"Why don't you put the gun down?" pleaded Jess, coming up before the low wall. "Tom, why don't you hand it to me?"

The moment with Sarah was broken, but it was all right now, for she had reached deep inside and rescued the part of Tom that knew how to live again.

"It all come back," he said as he lowered the weapon and stared into Jess's eyes. "She was gone. 'Fore I ever got a chance to pull the trigger, my Sarah, she was gone."

"Tom? That mean you—"

"Means I ain't leavin' you, son. That's what it means."

A great wave of relief flooded Jess's face, and Tom suspected that it went all the way back to when he had been eight years old.

"Tom, you don't have no idea how good it feels to have you say that. No idea at all."

Hoofbeats rose up behind, and Tom turned with Jess to look past Liz Anne and see Gabe and Sorrels ride up, leading a couple of horses.

"Mighty good to have you back, Miss Liz Anne," said Gabe with a tip of his floppy hat. "Figure you and Tom'll be needin' these broncs more than them dead men will. Jess, ain't the TP tracks a few days' ride upriver? Ol' swaybacked nag here's wearin' on me like a ugly bonnet."

Tom stood and started after Jess for the horses. When he reached the stacked bricks of adobe rising waist-high, he gave Sarah's grave a last look and prepared to climb over. The instant he placed a hand on the grainy top, a sudden constriction seized his chest.

Tom doubled over, the debilitating pain spreading like an ever-tightening band around the full circumference of his torso. He fell across the wall, disintegrating it even more, then it collapsed with him and he joined his Army revolver on the ground.

"He's down, Jess!" exclaimed Gabe.

The shadows of two men suddenly covered Tom, and he could hear Jess's voice frantically calling his name and asking if there was anything they could do. But this was the spell that Tom had been expecting for a long while, and it was all a matter of enduring and waiting, not knowing on which side of life he would open his eyes.

It took twenty minutes this time—twenty minutes that were like those twenty years—but finally the constriction eased, releasing Tom one more time just when he thought it never would.

Jess was there with a hand under his shoulder, and Gabe too, lifting him to his feet.

"Sure you can do this, Tom?" pressed Jess. "We

can get in the shade of these walls, rest all day if we got to."

"Just help me on a horse, son," Tom managed. "That's all I need, just my boots in the stirrups."

Jess reluctantly complied, and once Tom was astride the animal he seemed to sit his creaking saddle a little taller, for his shoulders no longer bore a crushing burden that had all started in this very bend of the Pecos.

"Obliged," he said as Jess handed him the reins. "Figure we'll be in—"

Tom threw a hand against the upper buttons of his linsey-woolsey shirt. He felt searing pain and heard Jess's cry, words that suddenly couldn't find their way across a strange and growing distance. There was another voice as well, maybe from somewhere ahead, but as Tom pitched forward toward Jess's arms, all he knew for certain was that it would be Sarah who caught him.

Author's Note

Although all characters are fictitious, this novel is based on three actual incidents in the Pecos River country of nineteenth-century Texas:

A May 1867 siege by Indians at Horsehead Crossing. Cattle drover Joel D. Hoy, his family, and several other men took cover in the ruins of the Butterfield stage stand and endured a three-day ordeal before their rescue by passing prospectors. One cowhand drowned, while Mrs. Hoy and three other drovers sustained wounds. See Patrick Dearen, *A Cowboy of the Pecos* (Plano: Republic of Texas Press, 1997), 72-74; *Joel D. Hoy v. The United States and the Apache Indians*, Indian Depredations Claim No. 2626; *J. G. Connell v. The United States and the Apache Indians*, Indian Depredations Claim No. 2618; and I. W. Cox to My Dear Children, May 31, 1867, copy in author's possession. Cox, a member of the Hoy party, wrote this letter at Horsehead Crossing immediately after the siege.

Tom Green's abduction of a teenage girl from a ranch on the North Concho River in the early 1880s. Green fled to Horsehead Crossing, where the girl's father, John Manning, (in the company of several other men) overtook Green, killed him, and rescued the girl. See W. F. Kellis, "Our Criminal Record Since Early Days," *Sterling City News-Record*, 24 April 1936, and W. F. Kellis, "Chronicles of Early Days," *Sterling City News-Record*, 11 December 1942.

Two cowhands' 1890 pursuit of Lorenzo Porez and his gang between the Middle Concho River and Castle Gap. When Will Landrum and Sam Murray overtook the Mexicans northeast of Castle Gap in an attempt to recover stolen items, Porez killed Landrum. Convicted of murder, Porez was hanged in Midland in 1891. See *The State of Texas v. Lorenzo Porez*, Midland County Clerk's Office, Midland, Texas.

Patrick Dearen is the author of nineteen books, including ten novels. A native of Sterling City, Texas, he earned a bachelor of journalism from The University of Texas in 1974 and received several awards as a reporter for two West Texas daily newspapers.

A recognized authority on the Pecos River country of Texas, Dearen has also preserved the stories of the last generation of cowhands who plied their trade before mechanization. His research has led to nonfiction books such as *Devils River: Treacherous Twin to the Pecos*, *Crossing Rio Pecos*, *The Last of the Old-Time Cowboys*, and *Saddling Up Anyway*.

Dearen's novels include *Perseverance*, the story of a young man's journey along the rails in Depression-era Texas, and *When the Sky Rained Dust*, set in the Dust Bowl of the 1930s.

He has been honored by the Western Writers of America, the West Texas Historical Association, and the Permian Historical Association. A ragtime pianist and backpacking enthusiast, Dearen makes his home in Midland, Texas, with his wife Mary and son Wesley.

Center Point Large Print
600 Brooks Road / PO Box 1
Thorndike, ME 04986-0001 USA

(207) 568-3717

US & Canada:
1 800 929-9108
www.centerpointlargeprint.com